THE KID WHO COULDN'T MISS

A Basketball Fantasy

Lloyd Harnishfeger

PublishAmerica
Baltimore

© 2006 by Lloyd Harnishfeger.
All rights reserved. No part of this book may be reproduced, stored in a retrieval system or transmitted in any form or by any means without the prior written permission of the publishers, except by a reviewer who may quote brief passages in a review to be printed in a newspaper, magazine or journal.

First printing

All characters appearing in this work are fictitious. Any resemblance to real persons, living or dead, is purely coincidental.

ISBN: 1-4241-3994-5
PUBLISHED BY PUBLISHAMERICA, LLLP
www.publishamerica.com
Baltimore

Printed in the United States of America

CHAPTER ONE

Marc faked left, then drove past the big Farland Hills forward and dashed for the basket. Just beyond the foul line he swept the ball upward and took his two giant steps down the lane. With easy, effortless grace he rose from the floor. He was flying! At the last instant he hooked the ball up and over for a perfect dunk. The fans exploded as this substitute senior guard scored his fourteenth point of the game. With blond hair flying, he hustled back on defense. A quick glance at the scoreboard showed Farland Hills still ahead by four with six minutes remaining in the game. The Paxton Pacers were eating up Farland's big lead with each passing minute. Most of the scoring in the fourth quarter had been by Marc. He wanted to win this one badly, and was playing like he had never played before! What a trip!

The Pacers had started the season well. Their first three games had been easy wins against little competition. This fourth game was a different story, however. Farland Hills was one of three favored teams in the Tri-Lakes League.

Marc had seen little action in the first two games, but had played nearly half of the third contest. While he still had not been named a starter, he'd been in several times during this game, and once again he had scored every time he shot the ball!

Farland worked the ball well, but Marc dogged every play, worrying their guards and breaking play patterns wherever he could. His legs were tingling and he had that funny, chalky taste on his tongue. He chewed his gum viciously as he darted back and forth following the play.

When their forward tried a shot from the corner, he zoomed toward the basket, knowing exactly where the ball would hit and where the rebound would take it. He leaped high as the ball slapped the backboard and came down with it clutched to his chest. Two quick passes sent the ball down-court and "Punchy" Markles banked it in. Marc shot a quick glance at Susan who was screaming and cheering in the booster seating area.

Slapping hands, Marc and Punchy, the other guard, back-pedaled fast as Farland brought the ball back on a flat-out fast break. With fine passing and effective screens, the white jerseys of Farland moved the ball into position for an easy jumper from ten feet out. Paxton was still down by four!

Marc took the in-bound pass and faked the Farland Hills defender out of position. He passed off to Punchy, then drove across center court his raised arm asked for the ball. Punchy rifled it to him as Marc went up for the shot. The Farland center was no slouch on defense. At six feet five he had a definite advantage. Marc rose higher and higher until even the opposing center's very long arms were unable to block the shot. Marc's leap was unbelievable! He soared up and up until he was alone in the air. With a soft, gentle flip he tossed the ball almost straight ahead and over the rim for the score.

This time, the fans were almost silent! No one had ever experienced anything like this. It was eerie. Had they really seen that? The boy's feet were at least three feet off the floor when he released the ball. Every fan from both schools knew that they were witnessing something strangely unreal. What could be happening?

Marc floated back on defense, a lazy smile on his face as the crowd finally got over their shock and began to cheer.

Marc checked the scoreboard again as he set himself for the Farland offense. His team was still behind by two with less than three minutes to play.

The worried Farland Hills captain called a time out as the Paxton fans screamed their pleasure.

Marc and his teammates jogged to their coach, grabbing towels to mop the sweat from arms and faces. "Biggy" Nelson, teeth flashing white against his chocolate skin slipped a huge arm around Marc as they huddled around Coach Crites. "Way to go man!" he grinned at Marc. At six feet seven and two hundred thirty pounds, he was the biggest and possibly the best player in the league.

Nelson's grin disappeared suddenly as Coach Crites grabbed him by the neck. By standing on tip toe and pulling Biggy's head forward he was almost nose-to-nose with the big center. "How many times?" he snarled. "How many times have I told you to stay between your man and the basket?"

"Yeah coach, well I uh." Biggy began.

The coach was not listening. He had already turned on Marc. His sweating face was on fire and his eyes were bulging. "What do you think you're doing?" he growled at Marc.

Marc dropped his towel in surprise as the coach tore into him. "Kelly was wide open underneath on that last grandstand shot of yours! Do that again and you're benched!"

The coach shoved them back on the floor as play resumed. Marc could hardly remember his coach's angry words. Already they were fading as he concentrated on the Farland guards, working the ball at center court. To Marc, everything seemed to be happening slowly. It was almost as if the game were being played under water. Every move, every pivot and pass was clear to him. He could almost sense the next thing Farland would do. He felt wonderful. he knew he could run faster, jump higher, and shoot better than anyone alive! Even the funny tingling in his legs and that strange taste in his mouth was not too unpleasant.

Farland's quick and capable point guard was trying to get the ball to his center at the high post. Seeing an opening, he set himself to slice a pass through the defense. He could not believe what happened next! At the very moment of release a blue-shirted blur whipped through the gap to steal the ball almost from his fingers!

Marc wanted to laugh. He snagged the ball out of the air and all alone, broke for the far basket. His dribbling was unconscious as with liquid grace he sped down court. At eight feet out, and with no Farland Hills defenders between him and the basket, Marc suddenly stopped. Not a single fan or player could believe what happened next. Flat-footed and relaxed, the blond senior guard pushed a gentle one-hander toward the basket. Both Farland Hills guards raced past Marc to take the rebound. There was no rebound. The ball arched up and slipped gently over the rim, tying the score. The fans exploded. So did coach Crites! Luckily for the Paxton Pacers Farland had taken another time out. If they had not, there would have been a technical foul on the Paxton coach. He was halfway out on the court jabbing a finger at Marc with one hand and pointing at the bench with the other. He was furious! Marc was out of the game.

"I told you!" he hissed, shoving Marc roughly down on the bench. "Why didn't you take it on in for the lay-up? There was nobody near you."

"Coach, I knew I could make the shot, so I. " Marc was starting to rise.

"Sit down!" Crites glared. "I'll teach you to listen to me or you won't play!"

"But I made the shot," Marc mumbled. But Coach Crites had turned to the rest of the team and was giving frenzied instructions for the remaining fifty-five seconds of playing time.

With Marc out of the game, Mickey Beeler took the point. Tim Wylie, Marc's replacement, was a lanky junior who usually played forward. Although not a good ball handler, the new man was excellent defensively. As always, Crites was depending upon Punchy Markles to handle the ball and set up the plays. The sub's job would be to help rebound and strengthen the Pacers under the basket. While he was not a starter, Beeler was a hard worker who gave Paxton good bench strength.

Farland brought the ball down fast as play resumed. Fans from both teams were creating a constant roar as the clock blinked its way toward the end of the game. The score was tied at 72 all, with less than thirty seconds to play.

Their guard, a flashy dribbler, easily out-maneuvered Paxton's newest player. He fired a pass down the sidelines and his teammate put it up. The ball touched the backboard, then caromed off the rim. Biggy Nelson went up for the rebound with the Farland center. Both big men came crashing down, the ball tight against Biggy's chest. The referee's whistle screamed, the sound hardly audible over the bedlam of the fans. Biggy was called for a body foul, his fifth personal. The buzzer sounded and the huge center walked toward his bench. Paxton rooters booed and stamped but it did no good. Biggy was out on fouls.

Farland Hills made the first free throw, but missed the second. In the struggle for the rebound the ball flew out of bounds. The referee gave it to the Pacers. Biggy's replacement threw it in to Beeler who was instantly double-teamed by Farland defenders. He managed to slide a bounce pass to Markles as the clock ticked on. Only a guard with Punchy's dribbling skill could pull it off, but he managed to wriggle out of the hot spot and get the ball across mid-court. Farland's man-for-man press was effective and time was almost gone. Coach Crites screamed for a time out but by the time Paxton called for it, only twelve seconds remained on the clock.

Crites was a good coach. During close games he always became too intense, and sometimes said and did things which got him into trouble with referees, parents, and school officials. Still, when decisions had to be made he made them and they were usually right. He had to make one now.

"Marc get back in there for Wylie!"

Marc nodded in agreement, a kindly smile on his face. Calmly, he jogged over to the scorer's table and reported. He didn't appear at all surprised that he was back in the game!

As play resumed, Marc passed in bounds to Mickey, then took the ball again on a quick pass. His mind was clear and his eyes and brain were functioning like a computer. It seemed to him as if he were able to see the entire movement of the Farland defense. Their coach had removed the press and gone to a tight zone. Both teams were doing everything to avoid fouling during these final crucial seconds. Marc hardly noticed the close but cautions guarding by Farland's front line.

Dribbling easily, Marc moved toward the three point circle. Almost casually he stopped and set himself for a shot. It would be the last shot of the game. As Marc cocked his right arm for the one-hander he was suddenly knocked off balance from behind. A Farland Hills forward had made a desperation dive for the ball. It would be

9

the biggest blunder of his high school career! The referee gave a mighty whistle blast as the Farland player grabbed his head in anguish and self disgust.

With two seconds remaining, Marc walked to the line. He didn't dry his hands on his trunks as Coach Crites had always hammered into them. Neither did he take his two deep breaths. As the ref handed him the ball he simply toed the line and flipped it up and in. He paid no attention to the roaring of the fans, all of whom were on their feet and screaming. The game was now tied! With a strange half smile on his face he simply fired the second free throw over the rim for the winning score!

For those who were counting [and quite a few were beginning to] Marcus Cassell had just made his thirteenth shot at the basket without a miss! What was even more amazing, a few knowledgeable fans realized that with tonight's game, Marc had hit the basket twenty-two times in as many attempts. He was actually shooting one hundred percent!

All the Paxton players raced back and away on defense, giving Farland Hills plenty of room in order to avoid fouling. Farland's in-bounds pass was snatched up and they managed a desperation shot from three quarters of the length of the floor as the buzzer ended the game. The throw was wild. Paxton won it by one!

Crites was jumping up and down, grabbing players, hugging fans, and generally going crazy! He knew that this fourth game was a crucial one, and they had won it in a real cardiac contest. Paxton fans had spilled out of the stands and were milling around on the playing floor.

Farland rooters were moving dazedly toward the exits. Their lanky center had slumped to the bench and sat there, head hanging. He seemed unaware of the noise around him. He paid no attention as a big hand shook him gently by the shoulder. When he finally looked up he was surprised to see the man he had battled the entire game. Biggy looked him in the eye but neither center smiled. "Good game, man!" Biggy said. He extended his hand, palm up. Gamely the defeated Farland Hills star tapped the offered hand, mumbled his thanks and slowly rose to his feet. He headed for the locker room without looking back. "They're never good when you lose!" He thought, as he dragged himself off the floor.

Marc was being mobbed! So many fans and players were crammed around him he could hardly breathe. They slapped his back, messed his hair, and some even tried to hug him. They were all screaming things but he couldn't understand a word being said. He just sort of let them bumble him around, a vacant, half smile curling his upper lip. He felt himself being pushed and jostled toward the locker room stairs as the activity finally began to subside. He didn't even notice when Sandi Myles, Paxton's head cheerleader, gave him a quick hug and kiss!

Coach Crites was still in a happy daze as Marc and the rest of the team burst into the "Pacer Pad" as they called their home court locker room. The place was a zoo. Players, fans, and even a few dads milled around in pandemonium. Steam was billowing out of the shower stalls and the place was getting cloudy.

Marc just smiled at everyone in the funny, dreamy way of his. At least a couple fans eyed the hero of the game with a questioning look. Was this guy wacko or what?

***

Susan scooted close to him as he coaxed the mustang into life. It was cold, and Marc's still wet hair steamed slightly in the dark.

"You were great!!" she whispered shyly.

"Nah."

"Yes you were! You won it for us! Everybody knows that!"

"Everybody but coach Crites," Marc mumbled as he backed out of the student parking lot.

"Is he still mad after what you did?" Susan asked in surprise. "You're the best out there. I'll bet you get to start next Friday night. Do we play Kirtland?"

"No we've got Madison Friday. Kirtland is Saturday night."

Marc pulled into Susan's driveway but didn't shut off the motor. He leaned forward against the steering column, his eyes half closed.

"Come on in," Susan said. She looked closely at Marc. "Are you OK? You look beat!"

"I'm O.K." Marc replied, but he didn't look up. His eyes were still closed.

"Come in, please," she begged. "I'll get you an aspirin or something if you really don't feel good. Dad and Mom are still up. I know they watched the game on TV. They'll want to talk to you. I do too."

"I feel awful," he whispered. "I don't know if I can drive home or not. Do you suppose I could call and ask my mom to come after me?"

"Marc!" Susan gasped. "What's wrong? Did you get injured in the game? What is it? "Something I ate!" Marc answered angrily. Then he seemed to fall completely asleep.

Scared, Susan ran into the house to get her dad.

Later that night she remembered. Marc had acted a little like this after each previous ball game. She was worried. She tried not to let her mind wander, but a dark thought was lurking there.

"I hope he's not into anything like that!" she told herself.

Three hours later Marc lay on his bed, sick and aching. An early November snow rattled his window as his mind rolled back. Back to the past summer in Mexico where all of this had begun. It was as if he was reliving those six weeks all over again....

CHAPTER TWO

Marc was plunging almost straight down. He could not stop himself, even by dragging his hands on the crumbling sandstone that filled this part of Yucatan. The hole that had opened beneath him was simply swallowing him up. His legs had slipped through, then his whole body. He fell only about six or seven feet, crashing down into what seemed to be total darkness.

He pulled himself up, trying to decide which part of him was hurt the worst. The hole above let in just enough light to see a little. Dust and dirt continued to dribble down, filling his eyes and hair. He started to cough. His left knee and elbow were scraped and bleeding, but didn't seem to hurt much. At least they didn't yet.

Peering around in the gloom, Marc began to forget his bruises. He was in a room! It wasn't very big, maybe a little longer than the distance from the foul line to the basket. Marc's thinking was often in terms of his passion, basketball! His prison was narrow, and the walls appeared smooth.

Even though he was just a *summer digger*, Marcus Cassell had watched enough of the archaeologists' work to suspect that he had fallen through the roof of some sort of underground storage chamber. Two others had been discovered previously in the area they were excavating. Neither of those was as large as this one appeared to be. Knocking some dirt from his blond hair, Marc took a few painful steps, sliding and stumbling off the pile of rubble that had fallen with him. The choking dust was not so bad as he limped further away from the opening. He looked around cautiously. The room was empty except for a small mound of squared stones which lay against the wall directly below the hole he had fallen through.

Twisting his arm allowed the seventeen year old to check his elbow again. A thin line of blood streaked through the dust. There was a large patch of skin missing, but no deep cuts he could see. His eyes now adjusted to the dim light, Marc stepped cautiously across the dusty floor toward the opposite wall. He kept a careful watch for snakes or scorpions.

There were no tracks or trails in the fine dust and sand he was walking on. Nothing moved.

Shaking his head in disappointment, Marc dropped a heavy piece of cut stone back on the pile.

"Just a pile of rock," he muttered aloud. Another look around was enough to convince him that there was no pottery, no statues and apparently no artifacts of any kind in the room. It was cool and dark. Not a bad place for a nap or *siesta,* but Marc figured it was time to get out and let the others know what he had found.

Even though he was an inch over six feet tall, Marc could barely reach the stone ceiling of the room. He tried climbing back up toward the opening but the dirt and loose rock only slipped and slid. *"No way,"* he thought. Still he was not concerned. The workers were nearby and the lunch break must be nearly over. He started to shout. After about ten minutes of yelling and throwing rocks and dust out of the opening, a shadow fell across the shaft of light from above.

"Hey Marcus!" It was Ignacio.

"What are you doing down in that hole? Are you playing basketball down there?" He laughed as he leaned across the opening and peered down into the darkness.

"It's another pit," Marc yelled. "You'd better see if you can get Dr. Spaeth. He'll want to see this before anyone else gets down in here. I'm going to need a rope or something too. I can't get out."

"Maybe we just leave you down in there eh?' Ignacio grinned. He squatted at the rim and tried to peer into the opening. All he could see was Marc's head. "Hey you got a lot of dirt in you hair, basketball man. You should keep yourself cleaner. If you don't, when you go back to the States that girl of yours, that Susan, may tell you to go back to Mexico and dig in the dirt!" He laughed again.

"Come on Iggy, get me out of here." Marc was getting a little annoyed, but he knew that the more irritation he showed the longer his friend would tease him.

"O.K. Marcus," Ignacio laughed, "I'll go get Tomas'. You are too big a fish for one little guy like me to pull out!"

Ignacio Villeareal, a student at Vera Cruz University, wandered off to find Tomas' and some rope. Marc leaned back against the cool stone and allowed himself to sink down until he was sitting. The scrapes on his knee and elbow had begun to sting. He dabbed at his cuts with a handkerchief. The bleeding had about stopped.

With the back of his hand Marc wiped the sweat and grime from his face and looked around again. Suddenly his eyes widened and his breath exploded in a silent whistle. Forgetting his bruises he leaped to his feet and slid to the far wall. Brushing the dust away quickly confirmed what his eyes had told him. The entire surface was covered with paintings!

As he waited for Ignacio to bring help, Marc's thoughts wandered back to the events that had brought him to this moment.

When asked what he wanted to be *when he grew up* Marc had always answered "an archaeologist!" From the age of seven he had hunted for Indian artifacts along the streams near his home in southern Indiana. Encouraged by his uncle Karl, Curator at a local museum, he had read extensively on the subject. As a result, he had become knowledgeable enough to be accepted as one of several helpers on this university-sponsored archaeological expedition. While it was the opportunity of a lifetime, Marc was unhappy that he was unable to practice basketball much during the summer!

***

Dr. Spaeth was a busy man. The newest underground chamber was now the focal point of almost all of the workers. A sturdy ladder allowed men and equipment to come and go. A piece of thick canvas was thrown over the opening to keep the sun's light out. A generator had been moved near and several heavy electrical cords snaked into the hole. The archaeologist did not want any more sunlight to enter the chamber until he had examined the condition of the painted surfaces. After all, no light had come into the room at all for the past seven hundred years!

Dirt and sweat muddied Dr. Spaeth's usually shiny bald head, and his glasses were coated with dust. He had been working non-stop for over fourteen hours. This third underground room was the largest yet, and of most importance were the beautiful, life-like murals which were even now being photographed from every possible angle. Several hours had already been spent painstakingly removing dust from the surface.

As the discoverer of UC-3 (underground chamber number three) Marc was allowed to help with the first examination of his find. It was soon apparent that the paintings depicted a complete and complex panoramic scene. Dr. Spaeth recognized it almost at once. Several figures were struggling over a round object about the size of the hands in the painting. Others appeared to be running and leaping about.

"It reminds me of a basketball game!" Marc laughed.

"Well you're not far off," Dr. Spaeth replied. "It is a game. The Aztecs played it on a special field. Thousands of people watched every contest, which often pitted one whole village against another."

"Sounds even more like basketball," Marc mumbled as he gently ran a soft brush along one foreground player's arm.

"The game was called *'tlachtli'*. It was sort of like a combination of basketball and soccer."

Dr. Spaeth pointed out a small stone ring that showed clearly near the center of the painted scene.

"They tried to get a hard rubber ball through this ring," he continued. "The ring was suspended from a wall, but it wasn't horizontal like your basketball hoop. Their ring was vertical. What must have made the game really hard was that much like in soccer, the players were not allowed to use their hands!

"No slam dunks then huh?" Marc said, grinning.

"Well they could only use their legs, elbows, or hips. What in the world is a `slam dunk' ?"

Marc didn't answer. He was puzzled. "What are *these* guys doing?" he asked. He pointed to several players who appeared to have something in their hands and mouths. Spaeth examined two of the tiny figures near the bottom of the wall.

"Looks to me like they're picking fruit," the old man said. He ran his fingertips along the painted lines on the smoothly dressed stone.

"They're eating it too," Marc said as he leaned closer to the wall. "Look at this one, He's putting something in his mouth."

A shaft of bright light flooded the cavern as the canvas covering was suddenly pulled back. Dr. Spaeth looked up angrily. "Hey! Close that hole!" he growled.

"Aw come on Doctor. Let me have a look down there. I almost found it, and I pulled Marc out after he fell in!" Ignacio was not that interested in the ancient burial chamber. Mainly he wanted to get down where it was cool! He had been moving dirt by wheelbarrow all morning.

"Alright," the archaeologist sighed. "Come on down, but close the hole after you. And only you can come. We can't have the whole crew down here at once. Don't touch anything." Ignacio was a special favorite of the archaeologist. The young man was intelligent and personable.

Ignacio was delighted with the wall carvings. When Marc showed him the two smaller figures at the bottom he frowned and moved closer.

"They are eating *malo hierba*," he gasped. "Most people will never touch those things. Grandfather told us about it when we were little. 'Leave malo hierba alone!'" he always said.

"I've never seen a leaf like that," Dr. Spaeth said, turning toward Ignacio in surprise. "Do they grow here?"

"They are very hard plants to see, but I can find them sometimes," Ignacio stated proudly. "One of my aunts claims there is one growing on the mountain behind her goat pens."

"Why would they be eating those leaves at one of their ball games?" Marc wondered.

"Well," Ignacio grinned, "maybe those two got lost and had to eat the *malo hierba* for punishment!"

"I'd like to see one of the real plants some time," Marc murmured as he helped Ignacio back up the ladder.

"Then come with me after work," Ignacio said over his shoulder. "I am going into the village to see my cousins. Veronica, my father's sister, will fix you a special supper. There is a dish she is famous for all around here."

"What is it?" Marc asked.

"Fried goat."

***

Marc grinned at Veronica. "Bueno, Bueno!" he told her. The goat steaks had been good. Beans and corn had been served too, and his belt was feeling too tight. It was a pleasant sensation. Ignacio's two cousins talked little, ignored Marc completely, and left soon after the meal.

"Let's go see if we can find the malo hierba before it gets dark," Ignacio said as he pushed his stool back from the table. Aunt Veronica looked worried.

"You know what old Juan Marco always said," Veronica told them. "I can hear him yet. 'Don't even handle that weed' and then he would spit! He would chop them out with his hoe whenever he found one."

"A silly story from an old man long dead!" Ignacio snorted. "Come on basketball man, we'll see if it is still there."

After a dusty climb halfway up the mountain, Ignacio stopped suddenly and took a few careful steps to his right. "Malo hierba," said Ignacio proudly. He pointed the toe of his boot at a small, gray-green plant growing out of a pile of rotted mesquite brush.

Marc dropped to one knee to get a better look at the dry, almost square leaves which appeared at the end of every twig. "Exactly the same," he grinned, studying the leaves closely. "They are sure enough what we saw on the burial chamber wall today!"

"*Si*! Didn't I tell you I could find some?"

Marc reached out to pick one of the leaves. His hand was inches away when Ignacio yanked his arm back.

"No! No! Senor Marc!" he hissed. "Don't touch them or you will die when the moon is full!"

Marc jumped back, as Ignacio started to laugh. "Go ahead," he grinned, "take some leaves. I picked some once and as you can see, I'm still here!"

"Well I know Dr. Spaeth will want to see these," Marc said as he began carefully removing the leaves. When he had taken the last one and wrapped them in his bandana, they headed back toward the house. Darkness had come suddenly, but they were guided by the yellow glow of a lamp which Veronica had set in the window. It had been quite a day!

***

"Yes, these certainly appear to be the same leaves as we see on the wall painting." Dr. Spaeth was holding one of them beside the tiny painted ones near the bottom of the wall. "I don't think I would want to eat one though!" he chuckled. He slipped the leaf under some note papers in the battered briefcase he always lugged around the dig site.

"Hey," Marc said, "maybe they ate these leaves because they thought it would make them better tlachtli players."

"Could be," the professor grunted as he continued to carefully brush dust from the painted surface. "Maybe it would make YOU a better basketball player this fall, eh?"

Marc shook his head sadly at the thought. "Maybe it would." He sighed. "I could sure use some help! I want to make the starting five this year. I'll be a senior and it's my last chance."

***

The summer was going fast. Marc had been busy at the dig every day. Even though his work was one of the lowest sorts, he liked it. He was burned brown by the sun, and the muscles in his arms and legs were bulging. He and another young worker had rigged up a round basketball hoop on a level spot near the dig. After a day's work he always tried to practice for at least an hour or so.

Four days before he was to leave for the United States he was looking at the malo hierba leaves again. He had pressed them between the pages of his Amateur Archaeology Field Guide. Almost without thinking, he began to chew on one of the dry leaves as he practiced short shots at the basket. After about a half hour, a frightening thing began to happen. His body felt light. He seemed to see objects clearer than ever before. Strength began to flow through his arms and legs the way his stomach felt when he drank Veronica's strong black coffee!

Marc's next act would change his life forever. Still feeling strange, he made a quarter turn toward the basketball hoop. Raising the basketball he carried, he arched a shot from thirty feet. It zipped through the hoop without a sound. He took the rebound and fired off another. A hit! He dribbled close for a lay-up. As he left the ground he felt like an eagle. Up and up he soared until it seemed that his eyes were level with the rim. He rammed the ball through and dropped to the ground. He had *never* done anything like this before!

Something was happening! Heart pounding, Marc stooped and selected a smooth rock the size of his fist. Picking out a small cactus some twenty yards away, he took aim and let the rock fly. It was a perfect hit! Part of the cactus was blasted apart by the force of the impact!

"Malo Hierba," Marc whispered. "It really WORKS! Wait till our first basketball practice. I'll show coach Crites!"

***

Ignacio shrugged, "Sorry basketball man, this is the only one I know of." They both stared sadly at the small pieces of dried-up vine that had once been the malo hierba weed. "You shouldn't have taken all the leaves from him for now he cannot live." He nudged the wasted stalks with his boot. "If we had time we might find another somewhere on the mountain. But why do you want more anyway?"

Marc did not answer. He had told no one of his amazing discovery. Twice more when he was alone he had chewed one of the leaves. The results were the same. For over an hour he *could not miss*, no matter how far or difficult the shot! Also he could jump higher, run faster, and pivot quicker than ever before. He tried to forget the blinding headache and nausea which always seemed to strike in the morning after he had chewed a leaf.

"My plane leaves tomorrow night," he said softly. "I guess I've got enough leaves anyway."

***

Doctor Gregory Spaeth's tent was only slightly larger than the others, but was much more comfortably furnished. Marcus assumed he had been invited there because of his *find* of the third underground chamber. Only Ignacio had kidded him about the accidental nature of the discovery. Dr. Spaeth had not commented one way or the other.

"Sit down, sit down," the archaeologist smiled as Marc entered the tent. "Move those papers on that chair there. I'll be done here in a minute."

"Thanks," Marc replied, trying not to stare at the prof's bare feet which were soaking in a pan of hot water. He glanced around the tent, taking in all of what appeared to be organized clutter. A hissing pressure lantern lit the tent with a harsh white light.

"Don't mind my feet son, but it's been a long day and they hurt!"

Marc nodded and smiled, watching the old man paddle up and down in the pan.

"I suppose you're wondering why I asked you over here this late. Well I thought you might like to be better informed regarding the mural in UC-3. It's in a remarkable state of preservation."

"Thanks Dr. Spaeth. I've been anxious to hear more about that game that's going on in the picture."

"Mural son, mural," the professor corrected him. "I think I already told you it is a representation of the game of tlachtli, a sort of ball game that was very popular all over ancient Middle America."

"I could see it was some kind of game right away," Marc replied. "I noticed that the photographer was in the chamber again today. Will you be sending pictures to the U.S. papers?"

"My goodness no! We don't want anyone on the outside to know about this yet. We'll need to finish all our work on it first."

"Oh, I guess I can see why," Marc answered. "Probably there would be a bunch of reporters around getting in the way."

"Well maybe," the doctor grunted, drying his feet with a towel. He handed Marc a small paperback book. "I've marked the section which tells about the game. You can take it with you when you go. I can tell you this, the Aztecs were what you might describe as addicted to the contests. They would wager everything they had on the outcome of a game. Sometimes they even bet their lives. If your village lost you became SLAVES to the winners!"

Marc whistled. He knew some pretty fanatical basketball fans back in Paxton, Indiana, but nothing like that!

"Remember that stone ring we saw in the mural?" the professor continued. "There were two of them set into the walls of the playing court. If one side managed to get the hard rubber ball through one of the rings the game ended right then. Usually though play continued until one team managed to get the ball to the wall at the opposition's end of the court."

"It must have been a real free-for-all!"

"I'm certain it was. Did you notice that the players were wearing knee pads, face masks, and so on?"

"Well I guess I saw that, but it's kind of hard to tell exactly what they are wearing," Marc said. "It looked like they had feathers and stuff on too."

"Yes, I know. Evidently they had pretty fancy uniforms since the game was so important to them." Dr Spaeth tapped the book Marc was holding. "Look at the photos and drawings of other tlachtli artifacts that have been unearthed. The game is very well documented, but I guess that the murals you discovered are the finest yet found. They will add even more knowledge about the life of the Aztecs and Toltecs. You are to be congratulated!"

"Me? What for?"

"In all my published work regarding this dig, your name will be used with regard to the discovery of UC-3 and all it contains."

"But I fell just fell through," Marc sputtered.

"Now, now," the Doctor scolded, "the actual METHOD of your archaeological find will not be reported!"

They both laughed as Marc thanked the professor and rose to leave. "I'll return your book tomorrow. My plane leaves at 6:00 p.m."

"See that you do! And Marc, if I don't see you again, have a good flight home. Thank you for being a faithful worker these last six weeks. Please drop the mosquito netting as you leave."

CHAPTER THREE

Marc threw another shovel full of snow on the pile beside his driveway. The November storm had surprised everyone. Saturday morning practice had been fun for once. Coach Crites had other business, so Assistant Coach Jamison had taken the session. A lot of the guys were goofing off a little and Jamison let it happen. It was a lucky break for Marc since he was still feeling sick from last night's game.

The driveway was about clear now, and Marc was slowing down on the job. He glanced up at the sound of a van turning into the path he had just cleared. A young, very heavy man climbed down. He was carrying a clip board in one hand and had a huge half-eaten sandwich in the other.

"Hey man," he called, "you Marcus Cassell?"

"That's me," Marc replied as he checked out the van. The letters W-PAX stood out in bold blue and white across the side.

"Quite a ball game last night, right?" The reporter had neither hat nor gloves. His pudgy face was red with cold, but he didn't seem to care.

"Mind if I talk to you a minute?" he asked. Marc thought the guy looked a little bored. "My boss sent me out here to do an interview. That is if it's O.K."

"Well I don't know about that, but come in. I've got the drive about done anyway," Marc replied. "This won't take long will it? I'm supposed to change the oil in Mom's car next."

"Nah, not too long. I'm Charlie Wade from W-PAX. How about we just get in the van? This wind is COLD this morning!"

They climbed in. Two technicians were in the back. After introducing them, Charlie switched on a small tape recorder. He wasted no time getting on with it. The technicians ignored them.

"I didn't do the live coverage of your game last night," Charlie said. "I had to do a lodge convention over in Lewiston."

"Too bad," Marc mumbled, "it was a barn-burner all right!"

"Yeah I heard," Charlie growled. "My boss keeps telling me he'll let me do some live sports, but so far no luck." He stared at Marc for a minute, checked the recorder, and then asked his first real question. "How many points did you get last night?"

"Sixteen, I think." Marc answered. He really wasn't sure. In fact he was having trouble remembering large parts of the game.

"Yeah, well the thing my boss is interested in is this. We've heard a rumor that you haven't missed a shot in any game you've been in yet. Is that true?"

"Well," Marc began, "in a way I guess it is. But I have had a couple blocked. So yeah, I guess you could say that."

"I don't care about blocked shots," Charlie wheezed, "I'm talking about times that you got the ball to the basket."

Marc didn't reply. He was wondering what Coach Crites would say if the interview actually appeared on W-PAX. Crites had very definite ideas about anyone on the team talking to reporters of any kind.

"Then you're telling me that you haven't missed a field goal or a free throw yet?" Charlie was making sure of his story.

"I guess so," Marc said, chewing on his lip, "but I'm not one of the starting five. I've never played a full game yet this season."

"How about in practice? You every miss shots in practice?"

"Sure I miss shots in *practice*," Marc said. He was feeling more uncomfortable all the time. Was this guy, Charlie, trying to trap him into saying something stupid?

Charlie wiped his face with a handkerchief. It was warm in the van. He turned the heater down a notch. "Well Marcus how long do you think you can keep up this kind of shooting? I mean, it looks to me like you're shooting one hundred percent!"

"I don't know, maybe ... "

Charlie cut him off with another question. "If you can hit like this why aren't you starting every game?"

"Hey, I'm not answering that!" Marc could just about hear Coach Crites if that kind of question appeared on TV.

"OK," Charlie responded, in no way upset. Apparently he hadn't really expected an answer to that one. The interview continued.

"Well," the reporter said, as he turned off the recorder, "I really think we've got a story here. Tell you what though, I'd like to do the video work in your gym. Do you think we could do that now?"

"Well maybe." Marc glanced at his watch. "The freshman team is probably practicing now, but they might be using the old gym. There's always somebody around to let us in."

Marc was pretty sure he was not doing right by allowing this interview without his coach's knowledge. Still Coach Crites was out of town so there was no way Marc could check on it. Also, he was more than a little put out at the way the coach was riding him lately. He decided to go ahead and do it.

The gym was chilly, but Marc suited up anyway. After a brief warm-up Charlie's two man crew began video-taping the boy as he dribbled, pretended to pass the ball, and took numerous shots at the basket.

He hadn't chewed any of the malo hierba leaves that day. Of course he missed several times, but made some too. The camera kept rolling as he tried some jumpers, lay-ups, and free throws.

"Well I think we got plenty," Charlie laughed. "Kid, by my count you took about twenty shots here today. You made maybe twelve or thirteen. That's pretty good, but it sure ain't 100%!"

"I told you I've missed some in PRACTICE," Marc mumbled. He was feeling more and more sure he was being used somehow.

"Watch the 11 o'clock news tonight Marcus Cassell," Charlie grinned. "My boss will have to decide if we show any of the shots you *missed* here today." He laughed and stuck out one beefy hand. "Thanks for your trouble Marc," he said as the crew gathered up the equipment. "Like I said, be sure to catch W-PAX at 11:00."

"Don't worry, I will!" Marc replied. I wonder if Coach Crites will be back in town by then, he thought to himself.

***

Coach Jamison set the straight chair backwards, his long, skinny legs splayed out like the roots of a tree. It was the year's third monthly meeting of the Varsity Christian Athletes Club. Marc, in the last row, leaned his chair back against the wall. He was not bored, as Jamison was known to face issues head on. Issues kids like Marcus and his buddies were vitally interested in.

"So okay," the leader continued, "before I turn the meeting over to Miss Compton, your V.C.A president (good humored boos) I'm asking again, what bothers you about some of the stuff we've been discussing in our previous meetings?"

This sort of question was used often by Coach Jamison. The varsity girls usually did most of the responding, but on this occasion the group was surprised by the deep bass voice of Biggy Nelson.

Well Coach," he mumbled, "What do you think. I mean what do you REALLY believe about some of that stuff in the Old Testament?"

"Like what?" Jamison asked, showing no surprise at all.

"O.K. like all those animals going into the ark. Do you think that actually happened?"

"The flood, Noah, and all that, right?"

"Yeah, all that," Biggy grinned, looking around at some of the other guys.

"Yes Big, I mean Mr. Nelson, I do believe that it happened just the way the Bible states it."

"They were all in there for forty days and forty nights? Must have got pretty smelly!" The group laughed, Jamison as well.

"Actually," the Coach replied, "it got a lot more smelly than that. They were in that ship for well over a year!"

"Man, you're jivin' me right?"

"Nope. Read it for yourself It starts in the book of Genesis, chapter 6."

"Hey man, I will," Biggy said softly.

"Thanks for your question. We'll talk more about this in our next meeting. Now here's your president. She'll conduct the rest of tonight's meeting."

The student leader took over, and the discussion continued. Marc, feeling a little sick as usual, thought about Biggy's question. Jamison's answer left him wondering. Was it all true then? He made up his mind to ask a question or two of his own at next month's meeting.

***

"Well here's the TV star!" Coach Crites crowed as Marc walked into the gym. Crites was standing in his usual spot about three feet from the out-of-bounds line. He liked to start every Monday afternoon practice with his own quick review of their most recent game. Marc dropped his gym bag and took a seat in the second row. He tried to hide behind Biggy's shaved head, but it didn't work.

The coach stood there slapping a clipboard against his thigh, waiting until the entire team was in and sitting down. Brian Kelly started whispering something to Tim. They both grinned. Crites gave them a look, but still said nothing. "Well here it comes!" Marc thought.

"Well men," the coach began, "we got a real break Friday night!" Crites was smiling! This alarmed Marc more than if the coach had been raging and stamping.

"I'm sure Madison's coach caught the interview on W-PAX last Saturday night. Our own 'Never Miss Kid' did just what we could hope for. If I know Coach Makely, he'll build at least some of his game plan around ways to stop Cassell. Well we've got a little surprise for my good colleague. Marc won't even be PLAYING!"

The coach started his review of the previous game without another word about Marc or the TV interview. The other team members avoided looking at Marc, but Biggy put a big hand on his shoulder as they trotted to the shower room to dress for practice. "Don't sweat it man," he said.

Practice was a bummer. Monday practices usually were, but this time several players were wondering why Marc's interview had riled the coach so badly. Still, he had told them specifically not to do any interviews unless he was present. Marc, they figured, should have known better.

The TV interview had been a real travesty! Charlie Wade and his staff had edited it so that only the shots that were good were shown. In fact they had put some humor into the piece. For one thing, several times they showed the beginning of Marc making a bounce pass, then panned around to show the ball going through the hoop. Practically everyone who was interested in sports at Paxton High had caught the interview. Marc had taken a lot of kidding during the day!

During practice Marc was again used as a second team stand-in. Playing against his first string team-mates didn't bother him much though. Over the past two years he had become used to it.

After only a half hour, Crites surprised everyone by cutting the scrimmages short. The drills came next, and they were bad, *very* bad.

"Intervals!" Crites yelled. A chorus of groans answered him as the already tired Pacers shot angry glances at Cassell.

"Thanks, 'Never Miss'," Beeler gasped as the hated drill began. Following their coach's whistles they sprinted the length of the gym. Spun around, walked five yards, sprinted again, walked, sprinted, pivoted, ran in place, sprinted again.

"Hamstrings!" Crites bellowed. The boys dropped to the floor. Sweat glistening on arms and legs. They were thankful to at least be able to get off their feet at last. Legs crossed, they straightened their left leg. Their right leg was bent, the foot facing the left. At Crites' command they leaned forward farther and farther until the tension in the hamstring tendon was severe.

"Reverse!" Too tired to even complain, they began again starting with the other leg.

"Twenty laps and stairs!" The team could hardly BELIEVE this! Frowning angrily they pulled themselves up and started to jog around the gym. They galloped on, turning up the concrete steps high into the stands, crossing over and down the opposite ramp.

Biggy Nelson slowed to a walk after eight laps. Driving his two hundred thirty pounds up those steps was taking more energy than his young body had left.

"Come on Nelson," Crites shouted from his seat at the scorer's table, "what are you, a WIMP?" Nelson didn't answer, but continued to walk as the rest of the team jogged past him.

"Easy coach," Jamison whispered. "The guys have about had it. Look at Beeler. Kelly looks a little sick too. And." The assistant coach grabbed Crites by the arm and pointed to the far corner of the gym. Marcus Cassell lay in a heap, a thin trickle of blood oozing from one nostril.

"Showers!" Crites bellowed. It was about time!

No one spoke to Marc in the locker room!

***

"Ready for tonight's game?" Sandi Myles asked. "Saw you on TV last Saturday night. You were great!" Sandi was captain of the varsity cheerleaders. Most Paxton boys thought she was the best looking girl in school. Marc could never remember her speaking to him before. He wasn't sure if she was making fun of him or not.

"I guess so," he mumbled. He almost told her he might not even be playing, but caught himself in time. If he gave this bit of strategy away, coach would really be mad!

Sandi was about to say something else when Marc's girlfriend, Susan, hurried toward them. Sandi gave Marc one of her famous dazzling smiles. Paying no attention to Susan at all, she reached up and messed Marc's hair. "Go get 'em tiger!" she said as she turned and skipped away.

"What did SHE want?" Susan demanded crossly.

"Who knows," Marc grumbled. "She didn't mean anything."

Susan's eyes narrowed as she slammed her books into Marc's arms. "I don't trust her, that's all. Are you driving me home or what?"

"Sure, sure," Marc replied hastily. All he needed was to have his girlfriend mad at him too! Susan was so possessive. Most of the time he liked her that way, but sometimes it was a little too much.

THE KID WHO COULDN'T MISS

***

Marc carefully slipped the two broad rubber bands around his by now battered copy of The Amateur Archaeologist's Handbook. Glancing up and down the hall, he made sure no one was near. For the tenth time in the past two days, he counted the remaining malo hierba leaves. Fourteen left. It should be just enough for the rest of the season. But what about tonight? Coach had made it clear that Marc would not be playing against Madison. But what if he changed his mind? If the game was close there was a good chance Crites would use his bench strength, Marc included. Still if he chewed one of the leaves half an hour before game time as he had been doing there might not be enough left for tournament play at the season's end.

"Whatcha readin'?" It was Sandi again!

"Aw nothing, just this book on archaeology," Marc replied. He quickly jammed the book into his locker and slammed the door.

"Well you be a winner tonight, hear?" she grinned. "The cheerleaders have a little SURPRISE planned for you. So be sure you don't miss!" She scampered off, cracking her gum and laughing.

"That does it!" Marc thought. He grabbed the handbook and shook out one of the now dried leaves. Putting it carefully in his shirt pocket he replaced the book and snapped the lock on his locker. "Please put me in Coach!" he breathed as he headed for the parking lot.

Thinking of Sandi, he was turning into his driveway when all at once he remembered that Susan had expected him to take her home. "Too late now!" he sighed as he slammed the Mustang into parking gear.

As Marc was running up the sidewalk he heard a shout. "Hey Ace, what's the hurry?" It was Charlie Wade, the W-PAX reporter again. His van was parked half into the street with the emergency blinkers flashing.

"You'd better be sure to watch 'Sports Round up' tonight at eleven," he said as he waddled up the walk. "I'm covering the whole Madison game live, and the camera's gonna be on *you* most of the time! We're going to feature you in our highlights section at eleven."

"You may be surprised," Marc growled. He stood on the steps, hands jammed into his jacket pockets. He didn't invite the TV reporter in.

"What do you mean, surprised?"

"Nothing," Marc snapped. "I got to get going. It's an away game and coach always wants us to eat early when we have a long bus ride."

"What does your coach tell you to eat before a game anyway?" Charlie was smiling, his head cocked to one side as if he were vitally interested. Marc wasn't fooled. He knew the reporter was only trying to keep him in conversation until he got something he could use. It sure wasn't the team's pre-game food he was after!

Marc decided to be polite, but he pretended to ignore Charlie's attempts to get inside. "Two poached eggs, toast, a couple bananas, soup and cottage cheese. Coach says we should eat at least a couple hours before game time."

"Do you guys use any of those sports drinks?"

"None. Coach says they have too much sugar in them and could cause stomach cramps."

"Sure, sure," Charlie wheezed. "Say, mentioning Coach Crites, how do you two get along?"

Marc turned a cool eye on the big reporter. "We get along FINE!" he snapped. "Why do you ask?"

"Well I was over at Paxton High this morning talking to some of your teammates. They act like maybe there's some bad blood between you two."

"I gotta go," Marc snarled. He yanked the door open, slipped inside, and slammed it in Wade's face.

"That you Marcus? Supper's just about ready!" Marc's mother met him at the door with a quick hug. "Why don't you help your dad to the table and we'll eat."

"Hi Dad," Marc said as he tossed his jacket on the couch. "How'd it go today?"

"Lousy! The computer was down almost all morning, but I'm on line again now. Help me into my chariot, will you kid?"

Marc carefully locked the wheelchair's brake. Slipping both hands under his dad's arms he eased him from the computer bench into the waiting wheel chair.

"Thanks Buddy. How was school today?"

"O.K., same old stuff. Adams is pouring it on in American History as usual." Marc checked his watch then glanced into his shirt pocket. He would need to watch the time. Since there was no reserve game tonight, the malo hierba leaf would have to be chewed up just before he got on the bus in order for it to take effect by the start of the game.

"Think you'll be in the starting line-up tonight?" Mr. Cassell asked as he wheeled himself slowly up to the table.

"I don't think so. Maybe," Marc hedged. "What are we gonna do about all the homework Adams keeps giving?" he asked, skillfully changing the subject.

"What is it now?" Mrs. Cassell sighed, rolling her eyes.

"Another term paper, and this one is due a week from today. I don't even have a topic yet and I'm supposed to have a rough draft in to the old slave driver on Monday."

"Don't call him that, even if he is!" Marc's mother admonished. Both parents laughed.

"Why don't you have Susan over on Saturday? She probably has to do a paper too," Marc's dad suggested. "You could use The beast if that would speed things up."

"Thanks Dad. The computer would help a lot but I'm not sure if Susan can come tomorrow."

Both parents had little more to say. They sensed that Marc did not want to talk more about Susan. Who could tell about kids? They sat down to eat.

"Marc," his mother began hesitantly, "I know how busy you are, and you've not been feeling well sometimes, but the oil in the wagon really needs to be changed. I could have it done at the station, but I hate to spend the money if I don't have to."

"Sure Mom. Saturday morning for sure!"

"Better slow down there," Marc's dad said.

"Maybe I was shoveling the food in pretty fast." Marc grinned. "Thinking about the game I guess."

"I hope you understand why we haven't been going to see you play," Mr. Cassell said. "these basketball games are just a little much for me and my old chariot here." Marc had heard it all before.

"Sure Dad, it's O.K., really. It's going to be televised live tonight anyway. Charlie Wade was here a while ago but he didn't come in."

Marc got up from the table and headed for his room. "I'm taking a nap. Coach's orders!" he yelled. "If I'm not up and moving around by 6:30 be sure to wake me."

The malo hierba leaf seemed to be burning a hole in his pocket as he flopped on the bed. Suddenly he wished he had never gone to Yucatan and never heard of the game of tlachtli.

***

Marc felt as if he was seeing the Madison game on instant replay. From his spot on the far end of the Paxton bench, he watched every pass, every shot, every move. He could sense if there would be a score almost the moment the ball began its flight to the basket. His smile was a little strange compared to the taught and screaming faces around him. Anyone watching him very long would surely have noticed something not quite normal in his gaze.

In fact someone *was* watching him closely. Susan studied him from the Paxton cheering block across the floor. While still angry about being forgotten, she was not about to let that get in the way of their relationship. She was angrier at Sandi Myles. The cheerleader's sudden friendliness to Marc had been pretty obvious.

"Marc really looks weird!" she thought as she studied his face. "He doesn't seem to mind not playing at all." Susan was worried. She knew him pretty well. Something was wrong!

Marc wanted to get in the game, but at the same time he didn't seem to mind sitting and watching. His fingers and toes were tingling again He bounced up and down continually.

Paxton was well ahead. The score stood 31-17 as the first quarter ended, so there seemed to be little doubt about that game's outcome.

"Punchy" Markles was having a great night already. Small and muscular he was making monkeys out of the Madison defense. He controlled his Paxton teammates like a field commander. Dribbling and passing, he set up play after play that dazzled the Paxton fans and kept the Madison crew rattled. In addition he had already canned two three-pointers and had at least four assists.

The second quarter saw Madison come out with a new defense, but after a few minutes of play Paxton had it analyzed and was rolling again. Markles and Nelson were especially on fire. The guard would twist and turn, feint and fake until he could fire the ball in to the huge black center for an easy score. Punchy even connected with two spectacular behind-the-back passes which brought roars from the fans. The half ended with Paxton still pulling away. The scoreboard read 55-37.

In the shower room the Paxton club was slapping hands and doing "high fives." There would be no problem with this game! Even Coach Crites had what looked like a smile on his red, sweating face. He began his half-time spiel.

"O.K. gang, quiet! Maybe you think this one's in the bag. Well it ain't! You let down out there and that Madison bunch can catch us in a hurry! Now listen up. I don't like what I'm seeing from Beeler and Kelly. You guys are loafing on defense! If we were playing any kind of a team tonight you'd have had twenty points scored on each of you. If you want to play for me you HUSTLE! I don't care what the score is!"

Crites kept at the two he had singled out. Slowly but steadily he was working himself into one of his famous rages. The team was used to seeing these, but they were still impressive. Nobody winked or grinned. None of them could tell who the next victim might be. Sooner or later Crites got them all!

With his time nearly up, Crites finished with a few half-hearted compliments on the first half. Then to no one's surprise he announced a different starting line-up. Coach Crites was not about to run the score up on the hapless Madison five. Doing that this early in the season would certainly have every team in the league gunning for Paxton.

It was almost a whole new team that took the floor for the second half. Paxton had good bench strength and there was little doubt that those second stringers would be able to handle Madison. Only Biggy Nelson of the first team stayed in during the second half. While neither Biggy nor Coach Crites had ever mentioned it, both were secretly hoping to see the big Paxton center win the Tri-Lakes League individual scoring race. Nelson was presently leading after the first four games. His average of 27.3 was only a point or two ahead of the next several stand-outs, however. With twenty-six points already, Biggy had a good chance of scoring in the high thirties tonight. Of course he would certainly miss the play making and passing of Punchy Markles. As the coach always said, "You can't score unless you have the ball!" This was supposed to be a joke.

Marcus Cassell was not sent into the game.

With but four minutes left on the clock, Madison used its final time out. They had managed to gain on Paxton's second team, and had reduced the scoring gap. They had effectively double-teamed Biggy Nelson and improved their own offense. But the Warriors were still trailing by eighteen points. Biggy's hopes for a forty point game were dashed, as so far he had only been able to add five to his twenty-six first half total.

Three Paxton players had not yet seen action during the game. Marc was one of them. Feeling good with his sixth win of the season virtually assured, Crites ordered the final three to report in. Marc was grinning loosely as he trotted out on the floor. The cheerleaders, urged on by Sandi Myles, started chanting his name. "MARCUS! MARCUS! MARCUS!" Some of the cheering block took it up too, with Susan yelling the loudest. Marc was not even aware of the shouting, but some fans, noticing his goofy grin, thought he was getting a little conceited. This seemed strange to them since the boy was obviously being kept out of the game for some disciplinary reason.

"He better wipe that grin off his face," one elderly Paxton fan told another, "or Crites will bench him permanently." The fan was more right than he could know.

THE KID WHO COULDN'T MISS

Madison brought the ball up court after the time out. Marc and J.J. Cramer, a third string guard, picked up their men. J.J. promptly got faked out of position. With a burst of speed and some classy dribbling the Madison point guard took the ball all the way in and scored.

Marc caught the out-of-bounds pass from J.J. and glided down the sidelines. The cheerleaders started to chant when he reached midcourt.

"Nineteen! Nineteen! Nineteen!"

Marc paid no attention as once more his slightly glazed eyes assessed the Madison front line. A tiny opening showed and Biggy spun around his defender. With one huge black arm, he signaled for the ball. Marc lobbed it high for the Alley Oop, but Nelson was unable to get the shot away. Sliding sideways two steps, Marc wove his way through the Warriors and took a short pass from Biggy. He pushed it gently against the back board for an easy lay-up.

"Twenty! Twenty! Twenty!" The cheering block members were flashing white-gloved hands as they chanted. With fingers open, they raised their hands twice, over and over again. Some of the spectators were starting to join in as well.

The W-PAX cameras were rolling.

Marc went floating back on defense. His long, easy strides made him appear slow, but in fact his speed was deceptive.

Moving in on the advancing red jerseys, he continued to smile. The Madison ball handler was good. A senior who had been an all league selection the year before, he knew the game. Seeing Marc's grin made him angry. It appeared to him that Marc was taunting him about the lopsided score. He charged straight at Marc, then dribbling behind his back, spun off in a feint. This was a strategy which almost always worked. It was beautiful to see. As the Warrior guard slipped by however, Marcus flicked one hand down past a speeding knee and slapped the ball neatly away.

The crowd roared as Marcus sprang after the loose basketball. He scooped it up running flat out toward Paxton's basket. As he closed in for the score, Marc picked up another blue and white jersey circling in across court. Slowing his speed a little he sent a lead pass to J.J. who took it on in. The ball circled the rim and hopped out. Both J.J. and Marc went up for the rebound. Two Madison players were after it too. Marc snagged it almost out of the hands of a Madison defender. He could have tipped it in, but instead brought the ball down and dribbled clear. As red jerseys converged on him he flipped a bounce pass between the legs of a Madison forward. J.J. was surprised, but managed to snag the flying ball. The path to the basket was clear. He took two dribbles and popped it in.

Madison controlled the ball during the final two minutes, and managed to score several times against the mostly inexperienced Pacer second and third string. The game ended with Paxton on top 82-69.

CHAPTER FOUR

"Well how did it go?" Marc's father yelled. He came wheeling into the living room as his son stumbled into the room.

"The Tri-Lakes League scores haven't been on yet. I didn't see it all, so I've been listening for..." Mr. Cassell stopped in mid-sentence as he took in Marc's white face and sagging shoulders. "What's wrong?" he cried. "You hurt?"

"Sick," Marc mumbled.

"Marc what is it?" his mother gasped, running to take his arm. She felt his forehead as she pulled him into the room.

Marc lowered himself slowly onto the couch. He let his head fall back and breathed slowly through an open mouth.

"How long have you felt like this?" Mrs. Cassell asked. Her brow was wrinkled with worry as her gaze darted back and forth between Marcus and his father.

"Just after the game I think."

"You were like this after last week's game too, weren't you?" asked his father. "I think you need to see a doctor. Something is definitely not right!"

"I'll be O.K." Marc groaned. "I've got to go to bed."

"I see we won again. What was the final score?" Marc's dad asked as he turned his wheelchair to face his son.

"I. uh. well," Marc mumbled. "Yeah I guess we did. I can't remember the score, but you can watch the recap on Channel 10. When Charlie Wade was here earlier he said they were going to feature Paxton tonight."

"You can't remember the score, but you do remember what Charlie said *before supper?*" Mr. Cassell demanded angrily. "What is going on here?" The outburst caused a painful coughing spell.

Marc shook his head slowly. "I'll be all right in the morning."

"Meg, call Doc Bennett first thing tomorrow. I want this boy checked out." Paul Cassell was emphatic.

"But Paul," she replied, "the school has a sports doctor on retainer that we can use any time. His name's Shelton. You remember him. Marc's gone to him before."

"No!" yelled Marc in alarm, "Not Shelton. I'll go see Doc Bennett if you want but I won't go to Shelton." He dragged himself off to the stairs without another word.

Doctor Roger Shelton, on retainer as team physician for the Paxton Pacers, was especially trained in detecting drug use by athletes.

***

Marc was still feeling bad as he and his mother sat in Doctor Bennett's office. As their family doctor, he had agreed to come in on Saturday morning. It was not his usual plan, which explained his unusually grumpy manner.

"Well what's wrong with you?" he asked as Marc sat shirtless on the examining table. "Your heart is O.K., reflexes fine, eyes clear. I can't see any problem." He closed the door firmly.

Marc gasped as the doctor plunged his fingers deep into his abdomen. "It's just that I'm really tired and sort of sick after every ball game," he grunted.

"How do you feel before and during the game?"

"Great doc. No problem then," Marc answered.

"You using any kind of medication or drugs?" The question was blunt and a little accusing.

"Heck no!" Marc replied, "I don't take any kind of pills at all."

"O.K., get dressed. Let's go talk to your mother."

"Did you find anything serious?" Mrs. Cassell's voice was quivering with worry. Dark circles under her eyes gave evidence of how little she had slept the night before.

"No, I haven't found anything at all at this point. My opinion is that this kid, like most of them, is just growing fast, probably eating too much junk food, and wearing himself out during the games. I'll prescribe some vitamins which may help."

"But he hardly played at all last night," Meg responded. "Paul and I watched the whole game on the late sports wrap-up. We even stayed up for the re-run."

"Maybe it's because he's trying so hard to keep on shooting one hundred percent in every game. Right, Marc?"

"So you heard about that too," Marc said, embarrassed.

"I sure did! I like to see my patients become real celebrities. It's good for business," the doctor laughed as he playfully punched Marc on the arm.

"What do you think we should do doctor?' asked Mrs. Cassell.

"Well maybe we'd better have our star ballplayer sit out tonight's game. You do have a game tonight don't you Marc?"

"Yeah we play Kirtland. I hope you won't make me miss it. I want to play. For another thing, Coach Crites and I haven't been getting along so great lately. He'll really be mad if I don't dress for tonight's game." Marc gazed earnestly at the doctor and hoped for a revised opinion.

"Well I'll tell you what," Doctor Bennett replied, "why don't you call Shelton. He's your team doctor, right? Shelton's a good man, and it probably should be his decision anyway. I'll let you folks and doctor Shelton decide."

Putting his equipment away, the doctor called to Meg over his shoulder. "How's Paul doing? I haven't seen him for a couple of weeks now."

Meg sighed. "He's awfully tired most of the time, but his job is a real godsend. He has three accounts now, and he can handle them fine right at home on his computer. He's not nearly so depressed, but he still doesn't want to go out much. He hasn't felt good enough to make any of Marc's ball games, so far at least."

"Why don't you have him call for an appointment next week. I'd like to talk to him too."

"Thank you doctor, I will. Thanks too for coming in special this morning. We appreciate it don't we Marc?" Mrs. Cassell prompted.

"Yeah. Thanks a lot Doc," Marc told him as they left the office. In the car, Marc made the tires squeal as he whipped his small white car out of the parking lot. His lips were set in a grim line, and he peered ahead at the traffic angrily. Meg held onto the door handle, but didn't say anything. She knew her son. Anything she suggested right now would only anger him more.

It was a very quiet ride home. Mrs. Cassell knew that trouble was coming. She also knew that her husband could not take being upset by family crises. She sighed several times.

By five o'clock Marc had won two arguments. He would not see the team doctor and he *would* dress for the game with Kirtland that evening.

***

"Yeah, I've got a question," Marc growled. The student leader looked surprised but Coach Jamison didn't.

"Please ask the question," Punchy squeaked in his high falsetto voice, "oh please, please, please," he piped.

"Knock it off Markles. Why don't YOU ask one?"

"O.K. guys," Jamison interjected, "get on with it Marc."

"To tell you the truth, I'm kind of mad at God." Marc looked around at the rest of the group. One girl looked a little shocked. Some whispering toward the back of the room stopped suddenly. No one said anything for almost a minute.

"O.K., so why?" Janet Compton asked.

"Why don't God show Himself?" Cassell asked, looking around at those near him. "If He's all-powerful as we're told, it seems to me like He could just appear and make everybody do right. You know, end wars, stop crime, all that stuff."

After waiting for a minute Miss Compton looked all around and asked, "Anybody want to answer that one?" Everyone laughed as their student leader's face turned red.

Grinning too, Coach Jamison raised a hand for quiet. "It's a legitimate question Marc. And you might be surprised to know it's been asked many times before. Check out Psalms in the Bible. Some of those guys were a little 'mad at God' too!"

"O.K. but," Marc began. A big brown hand settled on his shoulder.

"Let the man speak, Never Miss," Biggy Nelson said.

Jamison folded both hands around one knee. "I'm not sure this will help Marc, but let's think about it this way. We know that God loves us, right?"

"I guess so."

"And how we know," Jamison continued, "is that He sent His Son to die in our place. Do you agree?"

"Sure I do, but I don't get the connection," Marc answered, frowning slightly. The room was very quiet.

"God wants us to love Him in the same way. If He forced us by appearing and commanding it, would that be real love on our part?"

Marc sighed, "I guess not."

"As a matter of fact," Jamison continued, "God apparently did try what you suggest. When the Israelites were being led out of Egypt after four hundred years of slavery, God appeared to them in various ways. But do you know what happened? They didn't love Him at all! They disobeyed time after time. The truth is we can't force anyone to love us. God wants our love because He deserves it, not because we're afraid not to."

"Mr. Jamison," the student leader said, "I'm looking at some notes I took at our last meeting. Remember, you said we'd talk more about the Noah's Ark question this time. Do you want to take over and do that now?"

"Well O.K. Janet. Sure. Is that O.K. with everybody?"

Hearing no objections, he seated himself on the front of the desk and looked them over.

"What I'm going to say may surprise some of you. You may not believe me either, but I am dead serious. Noah's Ark still exists!"

No one laughed, but there were some grins. Several kids checked each other out to see how they were taking this.

"I'm not one to pop off without being able to back up what I say," Coach Jamison continued. "I'd like to share some of my research on the subject. Because you see at one time I had the same kinds of questions that some of you do. After all it IS incredible."

Jamison pushed his glasses further back on his nose and grinned at them. "Well here goes! The fact is the Ark has been seen many times since it came to rest on Mount Ararat. Marco Polo described a visit to the site during his travels toward the Orient."

He glanced at his watch, then continued. "I see it's getting late so I'll just hit the high points, but I'd be glad to talk more about this later to any of you who is interested."

"Go on, we've got time. You're not going to get out of this that easily!"

"Well O.K. Maybe you know that the Ark came to rest on Mount Ararat. I'm SURE it's still there, but that mountain is right on the border between several nations, so it's a very sensitive area politically. You can't just get your hiking boots on and go up there. Also, Mount Ararat is over seventeen thousand feet high, and very unstable because of earthquakes in the region. On top of that, the peak supports a huge glacier."

"Why not just fly over and take pictures?" one of the guys asked.

"Actually that's been done. The first time was in 1915 when a Russian aviator spotted the Ark from the air. When the word got out, an expedition was mounted. A group of Russian soldiers made it to the site. Photos were taken and everything. The pictures were sent back to Moscow by special courier, but the Russian revolution started then. The photos have never been found."

"Lately satellite photos have indicated something on the mountain too, but the ship appears to be in pieces. Also, much of it seems to have sunk under the glacier ice. Most sightings in recent times occur after especially hot summers which cause the glacier to recede somewhat."

"You sure you want me to go on?"

"Go ahead man, Mom will feed the chickens!" A shout of laughter went up, as everyone knew Beeler lived in a town house, and probably never fed a chicken in his life!

"Well O.K., but I'll just mention a couple of books that may help convince you that the Ark is still up there for sure. They're probably in the library, or I'd be glad to loan my copies out. One is NOAH'S ARK: FACT OR FABLE? by Violet Cummings. Another is NOAH'S ARK: I TOUCHED IT by Fernand Navarra."

"The one by Navarra is really neat. This French guy, Navarra, couldn't get permission to search for the Ark, so he brought his young son along and told the authorities they were going on a picnic! He and his son brought down a four foot section of wood which had been shaped by man. It was carbon dated at over 4000 years old!"

"There are lots of other books on the subject too, if you're still interested."

"But why hasn't it been found and pictures put on TV?" someone asked.

"I don't think God is READY for it to be made public yet. I'm sure though that when the time is right He will reveal it. What better way would there be to prove that the Bible is true? It will be the greatest archaeological discovery of all time! Until God's time is right I guess you could say that the Ark is in `cold storage`!" Groans!

The meeting ended shortly after. Marc headed toward the locker room, lips pursed in deep thought.

***

Coach Crites finished his pre-game pep talk with a surprising burst of praise for his Paxton Pacers. He was feeling good. The Pacer Athletic boosters had met that morning. They had complimented him on the team's success so far and, more significantly, had been positive about Crites' handling of the ball club.

Only one thing had marred the breakfast meeting. As the committee was leaving the school cafeteria, George Nelson, Biggy's dad, had asked Coach Crites for a few minutes of private discussion. Crites was quick to agree. He had great respect for Benjamin's father. [Biggy's parents steadfastly refused to acknowledge their son's nickname!]

"Coach," the tall black man had begun that morning, "is there a problem with Marc Cassell? He looks mighty good out there most of the time. You know I'm not one to interfere, or try to tell a man his job, but some of us have been wondering."

"Well," Crites hedged, "mostly it's an attitude problem. He forgets, or says he does, what I tell him to do. I just can't have that George. Surely you can see that can't you?"

"Sure coach. Believe me I see your problem, but that kid has great moves. He could really be the key for the Pacers this season. Have you tried just setting him down and having what we used to call a 'man-to-man talk'?"

"Well not exactly, George, I guess I haven't. But I've talked to him a lot at practice."

"I'm sure you have," George replied, straight-faced. He could well imagine the kind of talking Coach Crites had done during his murderous practice sessions!

"Maybe I can get a little time with him before tonight's game," Crites said as Mr. Nelson carried his cup back to the kitchen.

"Well good luck Coach. If I can help let me know."

Putting the morning meeting out of his thoughts, Coach Crites give his team a final jolt, and they burst out of the locker room ready to play!

He grabbed Marc's arm as he jumped up with the team.

"How do you feel about being on the starting team tonight?" he asked as the yelling faded out onto the playing floor.

"Thanks Coach," Marc smiled. "I really like to play."

Crites stared at the kid for a moment. "Is that ALL? You LIKE to play?" He could feel his blood pressure rising already, but he fought his temper until he could speak normally.

"Listen Cassell, how much playing you do is up to you. Do what I tell you and you could see plenty of action. Keep going your own way and you'll see action too, but you'll be seeing it from the bench!"

"O.K. Coach." Marc had already turned toward the gym door so Crites did not see the familiar grin on his face.

Marc was hardly aware of the crowd reaction when he was introduced along with the other starters. The Paxton fans were eager for some more surprises from the "Never Miss Kid."

Biggy got the opening tip-off and the game was under way. Within the first three minutes it became obvious that this contest would not be a repeat of their easy victory over Madison! Kirtland was big and fast. Also, they believed in a very physical style of play. They jumped out to an early lead, having tallied seven points before the Pacers were able to get on the scoreboard.

Biggy and Mickey Beeler were getting knocked around under the basket. Elbows were flying. Rebounding was murder as the whole Mustang back line converged on the bucket after every Paxton shot.

Marc was playing loose and easy as he and Punchy tried to work the ball and get control of the game. Marc's passes were so fast and hard however that several times Beeler and the other forward, Brian Kelly, had been unable to hang onto them. When Kirtland scored two more quick baskets, Punchy called for a time out. The score was 11-3.

Crites' previous good humor was no longer in evidence! In the middle of the huddle, he whirled around the circle screaming in the faces of each player in turn. His eyes were bulging and his face and neck resembled a ripe tomato. What he was shouting was right, however. He had quickly seen the basic problem and was giving instructions to get the game going his way.

"Cassell, settle *down* out there," he snarled, "you don't have to knock our guys down with your passes. Lighten up!"

Marc smiled quietly and watched the coach continue gnawing on his teammates until the buzzer called them back into action. He felt good. The sickness of the night before was forgotten. His legs were tingling and his tongue had that by now familiar chalky taste. The score did not bother him. He could only think about playing the game. He promptly forgot Crites' instructions.

Play resumed with Marc passing in to Punchy. Markles flipped that ball back and Marcus was off down the sideline. Before the Mustang guard could close with him, Cassell went high for the jumper. It was at least a thirty foot shot. The Paxton home court rooters went wild as the ball stripped the cords for the three pointer. As the Mustangs put the ball in play, Marc flashed into their midst.

Instead of slipping back on defense as he had been taught, he helped Biggy and Brian double team the Mustang guard. As the harried player searched desperately for any red jersey, Marc floated in and punched the ball neatly out of his hands. With two quick steps he retrieved the ball, spun around and layed it in. Brian was holding his side. He had taken a vicious jab with an elbow.

"Twenty-four! Twenty-four! Twenty-four!" The cheerleaders had not forgotten. They were leading the cheering block in acknowledging Marc's twenty-fourth clear shot at the basket without a miss.

Smiling sweetly, Marc trotted back on defense. His eyes were wide and clear and his basketball-wise mind was working overtime. Several times he leaped up and down with the sheer joy of the strength he felt. The crowd (unlike Coach Crites) loved it. Marcus Cassell was on a roll!

Paxton battled back and by the end of the first quarter they were only down by four. Marc had scored another three-pointer and the rest of the Pacers were starting to click. The holding, tripping, and body slams were increasing.

Assistant Coach Jamison took the huddle. Crites had cornered the referee and was reading him out!

"What's the matter with you jerks?" he shouted as he jabbed a finger into the striped shirt. "My guys are getting CLOBBERED underneath! Can't you see that?"

"Easy coach," the small, balding ref replied. "You get loud with me and I'll put a technical foul on you. I mean it!"

"Well look UNDERNEATH once in a while will you?"

The other referee was moving closer, sensing possible trouble. "Got a problem Bill?" he asked, giving Crites the eye.

"No problem, no problem. Coach here thinks his guys are getting too much contact."

"No *problem*? Coach Crites screamed. "Are you guys BLIND? My center is getting punched, kicked, and elbowed! I want it STOPPED!"

Fans from both teams were starting to get into it too. Kirtland rooters were booing Crites, while Paxton supporters were getting on the referees. The situation was building fast. It was beginning to get ugly.

"Look bud," the larger referee growled into Coach Crites' face, "we're in charge of this game and we'll decide what is allowed and what ain't! In the meantime you can sit down and shut up or you're *out of here!*"

"Oh yeah? You better not even think about kicking me out of this game!" Crites was gasping for breath. He was so mad he could hardly breathe.

Larry Crane, Paxton's athletic director, was on his feet and running out on the floor. Someone in the crowd hurled a tennis shoe which nearly hit the smaller referee. Crane knew he had to get Crites back to the bench before there was serious trouble. Grabbing him by the arm, he started pulling the still raging coach toward Paxton's bench. It was then that he saw the real problem. Biggy, Kelly, and Beeler were charging across court toward the Mustang's bench. The remaining Paxton team members were jumping up to follow. Kirtland players were spilling off their bench to meet them. Several fans from both sides were starting to move as well. In another minute things would be completely out of hand!

Two security guards dashed onto the floor and managed to get between the two teams. Back to back, they held their night sticks at the ready. Kirtland's coaches rushed in to help the cops as well. Nelson and Beeler stopped and glared at the Mustangs. Crane and Paxton's assistant coach shoved them physically back to their own bench. Grumbling and threatening they finally huddled up. The situation should have been over and would have been except for an unfortunate circumstance.

Coach Crites, although he had actually calmed down considerably, was determined to have the last word. The gym had been in an uproar for several minutes, but as sometimes happens, it suddenly became almost quiet. Nearly everyone in the room heard Crites' parting shot.

"That there," he bellowed, "is what happens when you've got LOUSY REFEREES!"

The refs whirled around. Looking like Siamese twins, both extended one arm and pointed straight at the Paxton dressing room. Crites was out of the game!

As things settled down the contest got underway again. Marc had not joined his teammates as they advanced across the floor to join the fight. Instead he had watched the proceedings with interest, a relaxed smile curling the corners of his mouth.

Assistant Coach Aaron Jamison, now in charge of the team, was a favorite of both Paxton team members and students. His classes in economics and political science were popular and in demand. His coaching style could hardly have been more different from that of the head coach. Where Crites yelled, bullied, and criticized constantly, Jamison encouraged and complimented at every opportunity. Together they made a perfect match.

Punchy and Marc worked the ball expertly as they attempted to draw the Kirtland defense out and away from the bottleneck under the basket. Several sensational passes had reached the black center and he had scored twice despite a lot of unnecessary contact from the burly red-clad defense.

Biggy was losing concentration. The pounding he and Beeler were taking was starting to get to him. Instead of concentrating on the game, more and more he was looking for opportunities to give back what he was getting under the basket.

Had Coach Crites still been in charge it is possible that what happened next could have been avoided. Crites was well aware of Biggy's toleration limits. The coach had almost pushed him too far on a couple of occasions. He knew all the signs.

Nelson had drawn his head low into his shoulders. His powerful arms were tense, and his right hand kept slowly opening and closing.

Marcus was dribbling easily at a standstill out front. He gave a sudden false start to the left, faking a mustang out of position. Changing hands with lightning speed, he swung to his right and drove toward the basket. Biggy was open. Marc's pass sped straight and true, but as the center took the ball he was slammed viciously by the Kirtland forward. Both referees were out of position and the body blow went unnoticed. What happened next, unfortunately, was seen by nearly everybody in the gym. Holding the ball in both huge hands, Biggy extended his elbows and whirled into his attacker. All the stocky defender saw was a big hard elbow smashing into his nose. He went down hard, blood spattering his jersey. Whistles screamed as both refs raced in. Kirtland fans had chosen to ignore the dirty work their team was doing, but they were on their feet booing and pointing at what they had seen from the Paxton center. Nelson didn't need to see the refs heading for him. He was out of it, and he knew it! Coach Crites was going to have company in the shower room!

Biggy stomped for the showers as the Kirtland trainer attempted to stop the blood from his team member's rapidly swelling nose. Paxton fans were howling too, furious at the injustice of the affair. But there was nothing anyone could do. More Security guards had apparently been called. They quietly moved along the sidelines, making their uniformed presence known. It was plain to everyone that the situation had become very tense for the second time during the evening.

Kirtland missed the technical foul. This, of course brought screams of delight from the Paxton bench. Things settled down a little then and the game resumed.

The Mustangs had a slim lead, but they were still confident. With both the opposing coach and the league's leading scorer now sent to the showers they expected to go on to an easy win. Not a few canny Paxton fans suspected that the whole series of events had been planned just to get Biggy out of the contest.

Coach Jamison had made several quick decisions immediately after Biggy's ejection from the game. Unlike Crites, he had enough confidence in his boys to gamble. New ideas and new combinations were what he liked! Without hesitation he had moved Marc to forward and slid Mickey Beeler into center. Wylie had reported in as the other guard. Jamison felt that this arrangement would allow Marc to help underneath, as well as giving him more opportunities to score. Unlike Crites, he was less interested in running disciplined offensive plays and more willing to let the offense develop naturally.

Luckily for him, Coach Crites was banned to the locker room and could not see the heresy being committed by his assistant!

The new coaching strategies were largely lost on Marcus Cassell. He was unable to remember coaching instructions anyway! In the first three minutes of play he had scored two lay-ups and made a spectacular block on the Mustang center. It was his rebounding that really delighted the fans however. At the instant a shot was made at either basket he was off. Flashing and weaving, invariably he seemed to end up at the exact spot necessary to take the rebound. Several times his astonishing leaps put him high above his taller opponents as he snatched the ball virtually out of their fingers.

"Thirty-three!" screamed the Paxton cheering section as Marcus sank a beautiful one-hander from deep in the corner. Thirty-three shots at the basket so far this season without a miss!

Marc's by now famous grin was shining as his latest three-pointer had brought the Pacers within four points of the leading but worried Kirtland five.

Some of Cassell's shots and tactics would certainly have landed him back on the bench had Coach Crites been allowed in the gym. The Never-Miss-Kid was all over the floor! He dribbled, passed, and faked the opposition to embarrassment. His defensive play was dazzling! The crowd didn't mind when some of his rapid fire passes went out of bounds. Seeing one of his teammates moving, he would rip a lead pass to the exact spot at which the player should be. Sometimes, however, they would stop or change directions and the pass would go wild. Two were intercepted. Coach Jamison was willing to let these mistakes go, in view of the way the boy was playing. Not only was Marc keeping the Pacers in the game, he was effectively filling the vacancy created when Biggy was thrown out.

Paxton was rallying. Beeler and Markles were getting open shots as a result of the havoc Cassell was causing for the defense. For the second time, Beeler was fouled as he went up for a shot. As he sank the second free throw Paxton fans went wild. With only seconds left in the first half the score was 41-40 with Paxton on top!

Kirtland scored again as the buzzer ended the half. Fans from both teams were on their feet applauding the excellent play their team had shown. So far, it had been the kind of ball game the fans both loved and hated!

"Way to go! Way to go!" Coach Jamison yelled as the team spilled into the locker room. Grabbing each sweaty arm he hugged and slapped hands with his boys as they threw themselves onto the benches. Biggy Nelson, seated in one corner, thought that maybe it was a little early to celebrate. The most important half was still to be played!

Coach Crites was nowhere to be seen.

The assistant coach was scribbling madly on the chalkboard. The offensive plays he was outlining were nearly the same ones the Pacers had been using, but there was one major difference. It was obvious to most of the varsity members that he was constructing strategies which would open more shooting lanes for Marcus Cassell.

The chalk broke in his hand as the Coach illustrated a final frenzied dotted line to the basket. Time was up and he sent them back up the stairs with a thunderous shout.

Marc floated out on the playing court. The Paxton crowd roared as he made three leaps straight up from the floor. Grinning, he swung his arms as he ran in place, pumping his knees high. Boos from the opposing fans were drowned out by Paxton's cheers. The people loved the exhibition! Marc, however, did not recognize the crowd's reaction. He was simply so alive and full of energy he felt he could not stop!

As the two teams lined up for the jump, Marc calmly walked into the center circle. Gently pushing Beeler aside he crouched slightly and eyed the ball. Mickey was confused. Coach hadn't said anything about Cassell playing center. The ref jerked his head at Beeler to move out of the way. He was ready to start the game. Beeler took Marc's usual position and the referee put the ball up high. Timing the jump perfectly, Marc took the tip away from the taller Kirtland center. He flicked the ball to Punchy who was so surprised he bounced it off one knee. The Mustangs took it down and the second half was under way.

Kirtland had won all nine of their games so far this season. No one had given them serious competition yet, but Paxton had them scared. During the half their coach had told them to slow the game down and control the ball. With Paxton's head coach and star center out of the game, Kirtland felt that by just playing good, tight basketball they should be able to win this one too. Their strategy might have worked except for one Paxton player; number forty-five, Marcus Franklin Cassell!

All the frenzied chalkboard illustrations coach had made at halftime were completely gone from Marc's brain. In fact he could hardly remember the change in coaches. Unhindered by plays and patterns, Cassell raced about like a demented person. Had Coach Crites still been in charge, Marc would have been benched immediately, possibly even kicked off the team! The assistant coach did nothing but watch in amazement as the senior guard-turned-center dribbled, passed, rebounded, and shot!

The fans were no longer calling out the number of successful field goals. They had lost count, but the official scorer had not. Disregarding blocked shots, Marcus Cassell had now scored forty-six goals and free throws in forty-six attempts!

Paxton pulled well ahead during the fourth quarter. The opposing team's slow-down tactics had been a disaster. The fired-up Pacers had taken advantage, and even though Kirtland had finally been forced into a desperate man-for-man defense, they were unable to pull it out.

The final buzzer was nearly drowned out by screaming Pacer fans as the game ended with Paxton on top by twelve.

Marcus had scored twenty-seven points and taken eighteen rebounds. His unconscious dribbling and lightning passes had completely riddled the opponents' defense. The fans tried to carry him off the floor but there was too much confusion and it never happened.

Sandi Myles, head cheerleader, forced her way to the center of the milling players and fans. Grabbing Marc's head with both hands, she pulled him down and kissed him soundly on the lips!

Susan brushed a tear from her cheek and stalked angrily toward the exit. She could not get the scene out of her mind. Sandi kissing Marc, and him grinning like he *just loved it!*

CHAPTER FIVE

Marc had been unable to attend church. Last night's game was a kaleidoscope of jumbled images which he was trying desperately to put together.

"I see why Ignacio's grandfather told everyone to avoid that weed!" he grumbled aloud as he tried to shave.

Back on his unmade bed, hands locked behind his aching head, Marc came to a decision. No more leaves! Having decided, he immediately felt better, but he was desperate to know what had happened in the game. Reading the morning paper had given him some of it, but still he could not remember the details at all. An ugly bruise was spreading on his left forearm. Where did that come from? His right ankle was swollen. It jolted him with every step he took. He slept for two hours.

The sliding door on the van wakened him. His parents were home from church. It was the first time Paul had felt well enough to go in several months. He knew he should go down and help his dad get into the house, but his ankle was stiff and he still had a sick headache. His mom would have to go it alone. She had done it lots of times, but Marc felt guilty just lying on his bed while she helped her husband get into his *chariot* and negotiate the ramp.

Marc pulled on a robe and hobbled down the stairs as quickly as he was able. By the time his parents entered the room he was sprawled on the couch. He had his twisted ankle on a footstool and was pretending to read the paper.

"Some game last night, right?" Mr. Cassell crowed. "Everyone at church was talking about you! Wow! We're PROUD of you son!"

"Thanks dad. Did you watch the game on TV?"

"Well what do you *think?*" his mother laughed. "We wouldn't miss that for anything!"

"Did they ... uh, show the entire game?" Marc asked cautiously.
"Of course," his mom replied. "W-PAX is really covering the Paxton games this year. They're even saying they're going to do the away games."
"I taped the whole game," Marc's dad said. "Do you want to watch it?"
"Boy do I!"
Marc's parents were surprised at how fast Marc slid off the co‍ ‍n and limped to the set. He re-wound the tape, pulled up the ottoman and planted himself two feet from the TV.
"Hey, maybe we'd like to see too!"
"Mom, Dad, don't talk to me for a while, OK?"
"Sure kid," Paul replied. "Maybe we can all watch it again later. I'll rest here in my chariot until your mom gets lunch ready."
Marc hardly heard them. The video was his salvation. Watching it should fill in all the gaps in his memory. No one would know how little of the night before he could recall!
I've got be sure Mom and dad get every game on tape, he thought as the action began. *As long as I can see it the next day I should be O.K.*
Marc's vow to stop using the leaves was forgotten!

***

Coach Crites was glaring angrily at his assistant. No lights were on in the coaches' office. The door was firmly shut. "I tell you Aaron, we just can't let him get away with it!" Crites' knuckles were white as he gripped his empty coffee cup in both hands. "You know I'm right! You let one kid start playing this kind of hot-shot ball and pretty soon they're all doing it!"
"I know coach. You're right, but ... "
"You darn betcha I'm right, and I'm gonna give it to you straight. You let me DOWN Friday night!"
"Well gee Crites, I'm sorry if I ... "
"You know very well what my coaching style is. Discipline, discipline, discipline!!!!" The coach smashed his cup down on the

table. "We've got to be together on basic coaching philosophy and procedure. If we ain't together, the kids get confused and they get hard to coach."

"You're right Crites. I agree one hundred percent. But let me say this; the Kirtland game was pretty unique. You were kicked out, Biggy was ejected from the game, the fans ready to explode! This wasn't your usual ball game, so maybe some unusual play was O.K. this time."

"I'll go along with that to some degree, but I'm telling you this right now: "Anytime you're in charge, and you let Cassell or anyone else run wild like that I'm looking for a new assistant!"

"Come on Crites. " Jamison began.

"Save it! We won't discuss this anymore. Besides, we've got to get down to the cafeteria. Man, how I hate these Monday morning booster meetings."

***

Marc pulled his jacket collar up against the early winter wind as he trotted down the steps toward the parking lot.

"Hey, Cassell!" A small, well dressed man called out. He was sitting astride a really beautiful candy apple red motorcycle. Despite the cold he had neither helmet nor gloves.

"You are Cassell, aintcha?"

"Yeah, what do you want?" Marc had slowed down but was still walking. The man was wearing mirrored sun glasses. It was impossible to see his eyes or determine his mood.

"I just want to talk to you a minute is all. How do you like the bike?"

"It's O.K.," Marc replied. He eyed the stranger suspiciously.

"Well you could own this machine right now if you wanted to."

Marc laughed. A used car salesman or something. This was a new approach!

"Get lost!" he growled. "I'm broke. Anyway I've got a car and that's all I need."

THE KID WHO COULDN'T MISS

"Hey, hold on, hold on! Just gimme a minute to explain. You can have this motorcycle without spending a *dime!* And you can keep your car too!"

"Sure! Sure!" Marc laughed as he walked away.

"I'm serious, friend," The man said, taking off the sunglasses. "Just give me five minutes to tell you how this works. It's about your scoring record."

Marc was intrigued in spite of himself. The guy looked like a creep, but he seemed harmless enough. "I'll give you five minutes, that's all," he stated.

"Let's go inside, it's cold out here!" the man complained as he lifted one leg off the motorcycle.

"Right here is fine," Marc retorted. "Start talking! Who are you anyway?"

"You can call me John, John Smith."

Marc snickered.

"Well kid, I understand you've made a bunch of baskets without a miss yet. Is that right?"

"I've missed some when they got blocked, or somebody pushed me or something," Marc answered, "and I've missed a lot of times in practice."

He glanced around nervously. No one was in sight. "Are you a reporter or something?" "But you ain't missed a clear shot in a game yet, right?" The man's eyes bored into Marc's.

"I guess so. What does that have to do with the motorcycle? Hurry up and get to your sales pitch! I've got to get going."

"Here's the deal, friend," the man who called himself John said, lowering his voice and looking all around. "All you gotta do is miss one shot on purpose and this little honey is all yours!"

"Hey what is this?" Marc growled, backing away.

"Relax man, relax!" Smith said quickly, "Hey, you're sure to miss one sooner or later anyway. Nobody will think a thing about it."

Without another word he pressed the start button and the little machine purred into life. Casually he flicked the light switch and touched the horn button. He grinned at Marc, his perfectly capped teeth flashing in the fading sunlight.

Marc couldn't help letting his imagination run a little. Strangely, he forgot all about Susan, but wondered how Sandi Myles would react if he came gliding up to her house on this shiny, red bike.

Seeing his hesitation, Smith pressed on. "See man, I've got big bucks bet on you, If you were to just HAPPEN to miss your first clear shot at the basket in this Friday night's game, the bike is all yours, clear title and all!"

"Great, just great!" Marc sneered. "And how do I explain to Mom and Dad and everybody else how I got this motorcycle?"

"No sweat, man! I've got all the angles covered. All you do is miss the first shot you take this Friday night. You do that and the next morning the bike is parked behind the sales office at McFaddin's Used Cars. That's over on the corner of Wellington and Brice."

"That still doesn't give me a reason to own the thing." Marc was getting disgusted.

"Let me finish, let me *finish*," John whined. "When you pick up the motorcycle, just look in the left saddlebag. You'll find the certificate of title all made out in your name."

"But. " Marc began.

"But nothing! There'll also be a typewritten letter in there saying the motorcycle is a gift from a grateful but anonymous Paxton booster. Now, do I have all the angles covered or what?"

"How do I know you'll come through?" Marc asked. He knew he shouldn't even be talking to this guy who was obviously some kind of small time gambler. Maybe even a crook.

"Have I ever lied to you before?" Smith cracked as he got back on the motorcycle. Marc did not smile. He thought about calling a cop but he didn't have much time.

"That's it, look her over," Smith said as the boy walked slowly around the machine. Marc had planned to get the license number, but was not surprised to see that there were no license plates on it.

"Well have we got a deal or not? You'll never have a better chance to get a free motorcycle," Smith urged.

"You still haven't told me how I can be sure the thing will be parked where you said. As I said before, how do I know you would keep your end of the deal?"

"O.K., O.K. you're a smart kid. I can see your mom didn't raise no fools! But I got that problem covered too!"

"How's that?" Marc asked in surprise. This guy was truly amazing, even if he was a crook.

"Since you don't trust me," John replied, trying to look a little offended, "I'll trust YOU! You can pick up the bike on Thursday *before* the game! Is it a deal?"

"Suppose I take it. How do you know I'll still miss the shot?" Marc asked.

"Don't worry friend, nobody welches on Come... I mean John Smith! If you take the machine and don't come through, I've got ways of convincing you. Like maybe a little accident with a certain guy's wheelchair!"

"Why you dirty. " Marc began as he swung around with fists doubled. But the motorcycle was already spinning away, the rear tire spewing dust and gravel.

"The machine will be parked where I said," he yelled as he buzzed out of the parking lot, "Thursday night!"

***

Susan nibbled at her hamburger. She had been pouting all evening, and Marc was getting very tired of the *silent treatment*. Still he hadn't brought the subject up because he knew it would be open warfare when he did!

Another painful ten minutes passed. Marc kept making slurping noises with the dregs of his soft drink. The straw was getting soggy and the ice was almost gone. Still it gave him something to do.

Susan cleared her throat. She did it again, then started in. "Did you like being kissed by `Miss Everything'?" she asked tartly.

"Who are you talking about?" Marc attempted to sound innocent. In a sense he was.

"You know very well who I mean!"

"If you're talking about Sandi, I had nothing to do with it," Marc stated angrily. Actually he did not remember. That had gone on right after the game, but some of the guys had kidded him so much that he had no trouble figuring out what had happened.

"Well you acted like it was the greatest," she snapped, "And you had that stupid grin on your face like. like you were in *love* or something!" Susan began to cry.

Marc started the car without another word. Actually he had expected the argument. They had had them before so he was sort of used to it! He was getting a little tired of the way Susan always had to own him! Also, his mind was on the strange guy he had met two days before. He cruised away from the drive-in and headed east.

"Where do you think you're going?' Susan sniffed. "I want to go home now."

"I'll get you there," said Marc grumpily, "but there's something I've got to check out first." He pressed the gas pedal and the Mustang leaped ahead. They drove in silence for several minutes.

"Why are you going down here?" Susan asked in alarm. "I don't like this end of town."

Marc ignored her and kept peering right and left at the vacant store fronts and empty buildings. No one was visible on the streets, even though it was only a little after eight in the evening. He slowed the car and made a right turn into an even seedier looking side street. Two figures lounging by a pile of broken cases eyed them suspiciously. Susan snapped the lock on her door and looked angrily at the driver.

"Let's get out of here. It's not safe!"

"In a minute, in a minute. I want to find the McFaddin used car lot."

"Whatever for?" she whined. "Marc, I'm scared, let's go!"

"There it is," Marc whispered. They turned slowly into the lot. It was fairly well lighted, although the sales building had only a token light inside. Doors and windows were secured with heavy steel mesh.

"There's nobody here now," Susan whispered in alarm. "Let's get out of here before we get mugged or something!" She had forgotten her anger as the immediate danger seemed ever more apparent.

"Is that somebody sitting by that little window?" Marc asked, craning his neck.

"For Pete's sake I don't see anybody. Just get us out of here, Marc!"

The motorcycle was nowhere to be seen. Marc whipped the car around the gravel lot, and bounced into the street. In fifteen minutes they were pulling into Susan's driveway.

They sat in the car and argued for another half hour. Her parents rather pointedly turned on the outside light. Finally, Susan ran crying into the house. Marc drove slowly home, confused, angry, and a little scared.

***

Marc was sprawled head down across the middle of his bed. His face hanging almost to the floor, he stared at the slightly curled brown leaf which lay there so innocently, almost under his nose. What to do? Coach Crites had announced the starting lineup for tonight's game at the end of the Thursday skull session. Cassell was starting at guard.

Marc was amazed at this turn of events, but he could not know that both coaches had taken considerable heat at the last booster meeting. The old guard fans wanted to see more of the "Never Miss Kid." Coach Crites was certainly not intimidated by the Boosters, but the truth was he had been planning to use Marc more anyway. Because of this, and politics being what they were, Marc Cassell would start for the Pacers!

The object looked like any other dry piece of vegetation. Marc picked it up by the stem and twirled it slowly between his thumb and forefinger. A few fragments flaked off the tips of the leaf. He had no doubt that without the narcotic effect of the malo hierba he would be just one more Paxton *bench warmer*.

In truth, he was enjoying the sudden popularity his amazing basketball feats were bringing. The sports editor of the school newspaper had interviewed him twice. Also, Charlie Wade from W-

PAX had called his home several more times, but he had not been home to take the calls. Marc's mother always assured the reporter that her son would call him back, but despite her constant reminders, Marc had not done so. Problems with the last TV interview were still painful. Marc was not about to let himself in for any more of that!

The clock on his bedside stand read five forty-two. The decision would have to be made soon. Tonight's game was on the home court, but there was no reserve game. He would not need to chew the leaf until a little after seven. This should give him the full effect just before game time. He couldn't decide.

The door creaked softly and Marc quickly shoved the leaf under his bed. Turning around he saw his mother peeking into his room.

"I'm sorry Marcus, did I wake you up?" his mom asked. Her concern for him was evident in the lines on her face. Marc suddenly realized that she was not so young anymore.

"No problem, I can't sleep anyway. Is there any pie left?"

"Yes there is but do you think you should eat it this close to game time?'

"It won't hurt. How about bringing me a piece?"

"How about getting it yourself if you're not going to sleep anymore. And Marc." she hesitated, "I don't want to bring this up, but your dad and I know your grades are really slipping." He did not reply.

In the kitchen Marc helped his dad move his wheelchair up to the table. They each took a piece of pie. Marc tried not to notice that his father only pretended to eat his.

"Wish I could go tonight son," his dad said. "I really think I'm doing a little better. Honest."

"You look better, Dad," Marc lied, eyeing his father's twitching leg and hand. "Maybe you can come to the Mayfield game. It's homecoming you know. We should win that one easy. Mayfield's really down this year. Everybody's beating them, which is probably why we scheduled them for homecoming."

"I'll give it my best shot!" Paul vowed, trying to make a thumbs-up gesture with his good hand. "By the way Marc, don't forget to change the oil in the wagon. It's way overdue!"

Homecoming, two weeks away, would not see Paul Cassell.

***

Marc looked pointedly at the empty chair on his left, but Susan, seated three rows back, pretended to ignore Marc's obvious invitation.

The meeting had been pretty dull at the beginning. Since the club president had a conflict, the vice president had filled in. He was not good at keeping conversation going. Furthermore the kid didn't seem to care much!

"Well if nobody else is going to say anything, I've got a question." Heads turned at this totally unexpected remark. Josh Lehman was a quiet, studious boy who in addition to his excellent academic record was a champion swimmer.

Vice President Gary obviously had no idea what to do. After a few moments of painful silence he finally blurted, "Well uh…. what's, I mean… what is it… well you know?"

Once again as the club's faculty advisor, Coach Jamison knew he had to step in. "I'm glad you spoke up," he stated, giving Josh a look of encouragement.

"Lay it ON us, Josh baby," Punchy squeaked in his famous falsetto voice. "Please oh PLEASE speak to us!"

"Easy Markles," Jamison said quietly. "Go ahead Josh."

"Well," the swimmer began, "I'm in advanced biology. Martin's section. I really like the class."

Some of the group erupted with boos and catcalls. Josh ignored them and continued.

"Well Martin says that all life forms evolved from more primitive ones. Even including humans. This is supposed to be a Christian outfit, so what about it?"

Jamison hesitated. He had been concerned that such a question might come up, but now that it had, there was no choice but to face it.

"Mr. Martin is a friend of mine as I'm sure most of you know," he began. "He's a fine teacher, wouldn't you say, Josh?"

"Sure he is. I already said I like the class. But you haven't answered my question."

"I'm a Christian," the coach began. "Since that's so, I cannot accept the theory of evolution. Knowing Mr. Martin as well as I do I'm sure he respects my belief even though it differs radically and fundamentally from his.

"Evolution is a THEORY. It can't be proven, since to become fact, a theory must be repeatable and observable under carefully controlled conditions. Since this is quite impossible, evolution must remain unproven. As a 'creationist', I readily agree that my belief in Divine creation can't be PROVEN either. I make no apology for this. It is a matter of faith, pure and simple."

"So O.K. then," one of the volleyball players interrupted, "you have a theory and Martin has a theory. Who's right? After all, they say their theory is based on all the fossils they can dig up."

"Good point," Jamison conceded, but let me tell you of at least one example where the fossil record itself practically disproves the evolutionary theory."

The session had livened up considerably! This was good stuff: one teacher not agreeing with another teacher right there on the Paxton High School staff!

"Did any of you kids ever hear of a big fish named COELACANTH? This is a fish which has four fins which sort of look like the beginning of legs. Lots of them have been found as fossils. Evolutionists claimed that it was a 'missing link' between fish and amphibians with legs. They also said that this creature had been extinct for millions of years. The only problem was that in 1938 a coelacanth was CAUGHT in the oceans off the coast of Madagascar! It had not evolved AT ALL, but was immediately recognized as the very same creature evolutionists pointed out as 'proof of the theory of evolution. Since that time many more have been netted."

"What did the people who believe in evolution do then?" Josh asked, leaning forward in his chair.

"Can you believe this? They simply said 'we've caught a LIVING FOSSIL" Jamison said, grinning and shaking his head.

THE KID WHO COULDN'T MISS

As it was late the meeting ended quickly. Jamison heaved a sigh of relief. It was not easy being a Christian sometimes. He hoped that if Josh or any of the others quoted him to Mr. Martin, they would get it right!

CHAPTER SIX

"O.K.," Marc told the bathroom mirror, "this time, but NEVER AGAIN!" He popped broken sections of the leaf into his mouth one at a time and chewed rapidly. As always, he couldn't notice anything right away. He kept on chewing until the entire leaf had turned into a thin paste in his mouth. He finished washing as he chewed, swallowing the goo a little at a time until he had it all down. After carefully brushing his teeth twice, he finished dressing.

"You about ready?" Mrs. Cassell yelled from downstairs, "You'd better get going or you'll be late again!"

Marc ran down the stairs and grabbed his blue and white Paxton jacket from the hall tree. He liked the coat. He had earned it as a junior, having just barely seen action in enough varsity games to be awarded the snappy looking garment. No one could miss the word "Pacers" arching across the back in large gold letters.

"Play hard son!" Paul tried to keep his voice strong, but the effort brought on a fit of coughing.

"We'll watch it on TV again," Mrs. Cassell said handing him his cap. "We'll tape it for you too if you want."

"Hey do that, Mom. I really need …. I mean want that game tape!"

"Bring Susan over after the game if you want to. I baked brownies and there's ice cream too." Mrs. Cassell yelled out the door as Marc climbed into the Mustang. He waved in acknowledgment and backed down the drive. Already he was noticing the *pins and needles* feeling in his fingers and toes. Marc was a little surprised at how quickly the MALO HIERBA was taking effect. He jammed the car in low and made the tires squeal as he sped away.

Leaves were completely gone from the trees and the smell of wood smoke was in the air. Winter was definitely here, but Marc noticed none of the signs of it around him. He was in his own little world.

With the driver's side window open the cold wind whipped through the car. It was unlike Marc to be driving so fast and so hard. He rocketed through two intersections on the caution light, then came to a tire-smoking stop when the third turned red. The radio was booming and he sang along, keeping time by slapping the steering wheel with his right hand as he drove with his left. Every block saw the young ball player getting more and more excited. By game time he would be flying!

"Too bad Mr. `John Smith' he yelled into the night, "you can keep your lousy motorcycle! I'm on a roll. Tonight I'm gonna score thirty points, and I'm NOT missing the first shot!"

The intersection at Weller and Sycamore, ten blocks from the school, was always a busy one. Marc saw the traffic light go yellow. Laughing aloud, he downshifted and stepped on the gas. The light turned red. A black mini-van was pulling into the inter-section, having waited for the green light. Marc saw the van pulling out. Just as on the basketball court, it all seemed to be happening in suspended time. He could even see the van driver's widening eyes and look of horror as the white Mustang came hurtling down upon her. Marc was not alarmed. Whipping the wheel hard to the left, he sent the small car into a slide. His over-active brain assured him that he would miss the other machine by several feet and slide right on through the intersection! He did not see the dark oil stain on the pavement. Earlier that day there had been a wreck at this same spot. Engine oil and coolant had spread out for several feet from the impact site.

Tires howling, Marc's car careened past the van just as he had known it would, but as he attempted to get out of the slide his front wheels hit the oil slick. Miraculously there was no close oncoming traffic at that moment. The little two-door slid across the center line, jumped the curb and sideswiped a lamp pole before lurching to a stop.

Marc unbuckled his seat belt and tried the door. It was smashed in and would not open. He slid across the seat and climbed out on the passenger side. The van was stopped almost in the middle of the intersection, emergency lights flashing. The woman driver, now nearly in shock, was walking unsteadily toward the boy who had almost hit her.

Marc was SMILING! The lady was furious, but before she could speak, Marc began.

"Hi! What a TRIP, huh?" he asked, laughing a little.

She could not speak. Was this happening? Could this crazy person who had nearly killed her and her two boys be so unconcerned?

"You stupid IDIOT," she screamed when she finally found her voice, "you nearly got us killed!"

"Sorry about that! Say, could you give me a ride down to Paxton High School? It's only about ten blocks. I'm in the game tonight and I'm afraid I'm going to be late."

The woman took two quick steps toward him. She stopped inches from his face. Her eyes were bulging and she was breathing in jerky gasps. "Not on your LIFE, Buster!" she screamed. "I'm calling the police. We're staying right here until they show up too!"

Several cars had stopped by now. Some to offer any needed assistance, but most just to see what was going on. One of them agreed to call the police on his cell phone.

Marc looked his car over. The entire driver's side was bashed in. It didn't bother him at all. In fact it looked kind of funny the way the fender was flattened and the door buckled inward! The rear window was a crazy quilt of broken glass.

"Boy Coach is going to be MAD!" he said to the lady. She was standing her ground, making sure he stayed put until the police arrived. "Our coach is a real tiger," Marc continued. He seemed unaware of the intense hatred emanating from the woman he had almost hit. She had started to cry.

"I'm going to get my van over to the curb," she sobbed. "You just stay right there and don't try to leave!"

***

Marc sat on one end of the long seat. He was tapping his feet and humming along softly with the music from a radio on one of the

THE KID WHO COULDN'T MISS

officers' desk. He had given them his driver's license and I.D. card. His parents had been called.

The officer looked up from the report she was putting into her computer. "No noise kid!" she said testily.

"O.K." Marc agreed. "Say, how long will I have to stay? I've probably already missed the first quarter and I was supposed to be one of the starting guards tonight too."

The desk sergeant stared at him angrily. "I said QUIET!" She did not raise her voice. She didn't need to.

"Sure! Sure! I was just asking," Marc replied with a pleasant smile. He looked at the large wall clock above her head. It read 8:24. The first quarter would be over by now. His smile faded a little.

***

"Marcus! Oh Marcus, are you alright?" Mrs. Cassell hurried up to him, pain and confusion twisting her features.

"Take it easy Mom. I'm O.K. The car isn't so great though. Can you get me out of here? I've got to get to the game!"

"I'm afraid you won't be able to get there for a while at least, honey."

"Why not"? Marc retorted. For the first time he was getting a little worried. Meg dropped her voice. "I just talked to the lady you almost, I mean the one that was driving the van. Oh Marc, she wants to press charges against you. She thinks you're on DRUGS!" Meg's whispering was so loud that anyone could have heard her.

Marc tried to grin, but it came out a little lopsided. Even through the euphoric haze brought on by the MALO HIERBA he had eaten two hours earlier he was beginning to sense the reality of the trouble he was in.

"Your father is in bad shape, Marc. You know he can't take this kind of stress and excitement. I didn't tell HIM, but they're planning to keep you here all night."

"All NIGHT?" Marc gasped. "But I can't stay here any longer. I've got to get down to the gym! I'm going to miss the whole game if I don't get out of here pretty soon!"

Marc's mother scooted closer to him and began to whisper again. The officer looked up from the folder she was holding and watched the two of them with suspicion.

"Marc, they said you should have a series of tests. They want to see if you have taken any. any." she started to cry.

"Any WHAT?" Marc said aloud.

"Any drugs Marc," she whispered, crying softly into a crumpled handkerchief. "I told them they could give you all the tests they want. Our son does not do any of that sort of thing!"

Marc did not reply. What was he doing here anyway? He remembered having had a slight accident with his car earlier, but the details were getting away from him. The chalky, bitter taste in his mouth and the annoying tingling feeling in his fingers and toes were the most real thing for him at this moment. He was unable to keep from tapping his feet.

***

Marc lay on the couch in the darkened living room. The ice pack was not helping. His whole head felt thick, and the ringing in his ears was maddening.

Meg Cassell got up and quietly closed the door to the dining room, which had been converted into her husband's computer room and office. She listened a moment by the door. When she was sure her husband was at work she hurried over to Marc's side. She sat silently on a low stool by his head.

"Marc, honey," she began, "don't you remember anything about last night?"

"Yeah, I remember most of it," Marc said with a groan. "It's just that so much happened I kind of get things mixed up when I try to put it together."

"Are you sure you didn't get hurt in the accident? Maybe you hit your head or something."

"Mom, for the TENTH TIME, I'm O.K. I did not hit my head. All I got was this busted lip, and my ribs are kind of sore. I had my seat belt on."

"Testing for drugs was RIDICULOUS," Meg whispered indignantly. "I haven't told your father anything about that, so don't you say anything either. It would just upset him more than he is. The tests were all negative anyway. I tried to tell them they were wasting their time but they wouldn't listen."

Marc breathed a long sigh of relief. His mother thought that it was because of his headache. Whatever was in the malo hierba was evidently undetectable in the tests they had used. He couldn't remember much of the testing either.

"Did you and dad tape the game?" Marc asked, moving the ice bag to the back of his neck.

"Heavens no! We were in no mood to think about some dumb basketball game. What with you in jail and everything." Meg replied, "Your team won though. You've had several calls this morning, but I told them you were O.K. but sleeping."

"Who called?"

"Well Susan about five times," Meg laughed.

"Well who else, Mom?"

"Your coaches both called after the game. Your father told them all that he knew at the time. He still thinks you were in the hospital all night for 'observation'. Coach Crites called again early this morning. I'm to call him back as soon as you are up. Marc, he said the principal told him your grades will have to improve or you may be ineligible to play." Marc looked away, his eyes squeezed shut.

"Did any of the guys call?" Marc asked.

"Oh yes, the Nelson boy and the one you call 'Punchy', And I almost forgot, another girl called too. She said her name was Sandi. You're supposed to call her back. She left her number. Yes, we've had phone calls!"

"Where's my car?" Marc suddenly blurted.

"Mr. Carey and his daughter went down to look at it. You'll need to call and thank them. He is such a wonderful neighbor. Mr. Carey said it was still drivable so Connie drove his car back and he drove yours home. It's sitting beside the Careys' garage."

"Did the girl that called give you her last name?" Marc asked, trying to sound slightly disinterested.

"No, but she sounded very nice on the phone. She seemed to be very concerned about you. Does Susan know about this?" his mother teased.

Marc did not answer.

"The team doctor called too," Meg continued. He has set up an appointment for you at the hospital today. We're to have you there at 2:30. Your coach said he will not expect you at practice until you have been checked out, and are feeling up to it. And Marc, you know you'll have to call the lady you almost hit. She deserves an apology!"

Marc took a deep breath and let it out in a long, silent sigh. It looked like things were going to be O.K.

He did not allow himself to think about talking to the lady. He had never had anyone this angry with him. An apology to her, painful as it would be for him, was sure a lot better than a lawsuit!

He opened his chemistry book and forced himself to concentrate. The time off would give him a chance to get his grades up a little.

***

"But I don't want to," Beeler whispered.

"Aw go on and do it," Marc whispered back.

"Hey knock it off you two!" Janet Compton was getting annoyed at the two ball players in the back row. "If you have something to say, tell it to all of us!"

Marc grabbed Beeler's arm and pushed it high. They tussled a minute, then without standing, Beeler nodded at their Varsity Christian Athletic Club chairperson. "What's your comment, Mr. Beeler?" she asked, putting a little extra emphasis on the Mr.

"Well. uh. O.K. uh," he stammered, "it's about my cousin."

Coach Jamison, their faculty advisor, was listening closely but he let Janet continue. "Tell us about it." Janet's voice was calm and compassionate.

"O.K.," he began, "Jim, my cousin, is in the navy. He's on a carrier in the Middle East somewhere. Or at least he was the last we heard. We're buddies. We write back and forth quite a bit."

Hands in his jacket pockets and hunched down so much that few in the room could see him clearly, he finally continued. "About two months ago he fell off the plane engine he was working on and he injured his back real bad. He's a mechanic, see? So O.K. We all started to pray for him to get out of sick bay and get well. But he ain't well at all. My aunt said he may never walk again."

After a long silence, Janet asked gently, "So what is your question for the group here?"

"Just about everybody I *know* has been praying for Jim. We're praying for a miracle, get it? But it's just not happening. Our pastor keeps shoving these Bible verses at us about miracles and healing and stuff, but. well... like I said... "

Janet pushed her reddish hair back from her forehead. "Which Bible verses? Do you remember any of them?"

"I can't say it exactly," Beeler growled.

"Well just in your own words is O.K." Coach Jamison was impressed with the young chairperson's tact in the situation. He remained silent but very alert.

"Just try," Janet coaxed.

"Something...something about if two people agreed on a thing they wanted, the Lord will do it."

Janet shot a worried glance at their advisor. Jamison spoke up, keeping his voice even and non-judgmental. "I think the verses you're talking about are in Matthew's gospel. I can't quote it exactly either. Chapter eighteen I think. Carol you're in the front row. Here's the little pocket New Testament I carry. Look it up for us."

After a few embarrassing fumbles the freshman girl found the passage. She looked at Janet, not knowing what to do.

"Read it to us," Janet said.

"Again I say to you..."

"A lot LOUDER please," Janet requested.

"Again I say to you that if two of you shall agree on earth as touching anything that they shall ask, it shall be done for them of my Father which is in heaven." Carol looked up, but did not continue.

"That's one of them alright, and there were some other ones like that too." Beeler's eyes flicked back and forth between the chairperson and Coach Jamison. "So why doesn't God do what He said He would?"

Janet was at a loss. She was just a high school student. There was no way she could respond. Hopefully she turned to the Coach.

"You know Mickey," he began, "your question has been asked millions of times during the history of Christianity. It might amaze you to know that Jesus himself asked for a miracle when he was about to die on the cross. 'Let this cup pass from me,' he begged of God the Father. But the answer was no. And we can all be eternally grateful for that! We can ask God, but we cannot DEMAND. God is God. He will decide what is best even if we can't see it at this time."

Beeler, unconvinced, shrugged but said no more. The meeting ended shortly after. Most of the kids left without the usual chatter.

***

Marc was not surprised to find himself riding the bench once again as the first quarter ended. East Central Tech was not a basketball school. Their football and wrestling programs were outstanding, but in round ball they were just not in the same league with Paxton.

Coach Crites had provided no explanation for not letting the Never-Miss-Kid into the ball game. The fans were not calling for him, probably assuming he still had injuries and was being given time to heal up.

For the first time in his life Marc was glad he was not playing. He had not eaten one of his eleven remaining leaves. If he went into the game without the malo hierba he was sure to miss a shot sooner or later. He sort of wanted to keep the publicity going. He would have died before admitting it to anyone, but he was greatly enjoying his new popularity. It was getting to be a very important thing with him.

Biggy Nelson was having another super night. Taking advantage of Central Tech's half-hearted rebounding, he was in almost total control of both the offensive and defensive boards. Two inches taller and some forty pounds heavier than the opposing center, he was scoring almost every time he got the ball. By the end of the first half he had tallied eleven field goals and four free-throws. He had even pumped in a looping one-handed three pointer, the first he had ever made. Coach Crites had started to scream at Biggy for taking the long shot, but Paxton was so far ahead his heart just wasn't in it. Biggy just turned and flashed a dazzling smile at his coach. Some of the more canny fans got a big laugh out of this bit of by-play. Coach Crites glared, but his assistant hid a big grin, behind his clipboard.

Even though it was a home game for Central Tech, not many fans had shown up. Tech was without a win in nine starts, and it didn't look good for the rest of the season. Even many of Paxton's usually loyal fans had stayed away from this contest. It was sort of a quiet game.

Crites used all but two of his players in the second half. J.J. and Marc did not get in.

J.J. was mad! "Why don't you put me in?" he growled, hands dangling between his knees. "He's used everybody else!" Realizing that Marc had heard him, he turned to the player on his left and started a quick conversation. Marc tried to look disgusted too, but it was not easy. He couldn't have been happier. The bench actually felt soft tonight!

The game was a lackluster affair. The Tech coaches and cheerleaders did their best, but the outcome of the contest was never in doubt. Many fans had begun leaving as early as the end of the third quarter. It was a slim crowd (mostly Paxton fans) who heard the final buzzer. Paxton had their twelfth win of the season. They were still undefeated.

Marc was also benched the next night. He was happy that Paxton won easily, but he had used one of his leaves in case he got to play. There weren't many left.

Marc had a good workout at Monday night's practice. His ribs were still sore, but the two game rest had been good. He was feeling fit. He wanted to play again.

Crites gave them his usual tongue-lashing at the end of the session. Admittedly their play had been sloppy and undisciplined in the Tech game. He knew (but didn't say) that it is hard to play your best against a very poor opponent. The Pacers had been much better against Sedalia but Crites didn't say much about that!

He targeted his big center for special abuse. Biggy took it well. He kept his eyes down, and on occasion shook his head sadly as if in true self-condemnation. Most of the team knew it was only an act. It was difficult to insult the huge senior, but it was very unwise to make him *angry!*

Biggy had scored forty-one points in Friday night's contest, but in the Sedalia game only 24. He had now dropped to third place in the league scoring race. Only a few percentage points separated the first three leaders. Biggy would need several more high scoring games to regain the lead.

The player Nelson was most worried about was Seth Caton, a flashy forward from Calbert Country Day Academy and only a junior. Sports writers were already comparing him to a young Larry Bastion.

Benjamin ("Biggy") Nelson had already decided that he, and not Seth Caton, would receive the individual scoring record honors! Let Caton have it his senior year. By then Biggy expected to be playing for one of the four colleges and three universities that had already been showing real interest in him.

The skull session over, Marc followed Punchy out of the gym. It had warmed up a little, but it was still cold. A raw wind came in off the lake. Punchy ruffled his curly mop, trying to dry it in the wind.

"Who's the creep?" Punchy murmured, eyeing the small, well-dressed man. He was sitting nonchalantly on the motorcycle. Both pointed-toe boots were just touching the blacktop. His arms were folded across the expensive leather jacket, which was turned up at the collar. A thin, scarf and heavy gloves attested to a cold ride.

"Oh no!" Marc breathed, squinting into the setting sun. "It's him again!"

"Who's 'him'?" Punchy wanted to know.

Brian Kelly was inspecting the motorcycle while shooting questioning glances at the stranger.

"Nice bike, huh?" the man who called himself John Smith asked Brian. The silver sunglasses stayed in place, and he hardly moved his lips as he spoke. The effect was almost that of a ventriloquist without a dummy.

Brian didn't answer, nor did he get any closer.

"My man, Marc," Smith said, still without unfolding his arms. "I need to see you a minute. in private."

"Get lost!" Marc responded under his breath. "You and me have nothing to say to each other, so forget it."

"Easy, man. Easy. We're cool. Get rid of the gang there and listen to what I've got to say. Oh by the way, take a look at this." Smith slipped an official looking paper out of his jacket and handed it over.

"So you did it, huh?" Marc said as he glanced at the certificate of title. It was made out in his name.

"All you gotta do, my man, is miss your first shot in the Jordan Valley East game and this little baby is all yours!"

"I thought the deal was for three games ago. And another thing, I drove out to that used car lot just before the game. The motorcycle wasn't there like you said it would be."

"Yeah, you were there O.K. Had a girlfriend with you, right? Good looking kid wearing a blue jacket? Came about eight o'clock, right? The bike was there alright!"

Marc was amazed. "Where were you?" he asked.

"I've got ways, Ace. I've got ways! The deal's still on."

"I heard about your brush with the law. Lucky you didn't get sued! Anyway, since you didn't play in the last three games, the plan now is for your first clear shot in the game you play in. I put a few more bucks on you too, so it's kind of important to me that the deal goes through!"

Marc glanced around the parking area. All the guys had left. A couple of young kids were dragging a sled around in the dirty snow near the end of the lot, but nobody was within hearing distance.

Smith carefully set the kickstand. The silver toes on his boots flashed as he swung one leg over the seat.

"Go ahead Ace, get on," he said grinning.

Marc dropped into the saddle. The handle grips were soft and the chromed instrument panel twinkled in the twilight. *What a machine!* he thought.

CHAPTER SEVEN

"Please Marc, I've got to know!" Susan brushed a tear from the corner of one eye with her jacket sleeve.

"I tell you I'm not doing drugs!" Marc hissed, glancing around the hallway. No one was paying any attention to them. Lockers were banging and the noise of kids shouting to each other was deafening.

"But Marc honey, you act so *weird* during the games. And what about those 'memory blocks' or whatever you call them? We studied the signs in health class last year. You've got all of them. And what about your math grades? You almost flunked that test yesterday!"

Marcus smashed his locker closed and grabbed a handful of her books. "Just forget it, OK? I'm playing pretty good ball they tell me. If I was tripping out don't you think that would not be happening? And how is a guy supposed to remember all that stuff in math anyway? It's worthless!"

"Please don't get mad, Marc. It's just that I really care about you. I'm worried is all."

"Well don't be!"

"Maybe I shouldn't even tell you this," Susan began hesitantly, "but you know that accident you had?"

"Well what about it? Nobody got hurt?"

"I know it, Marc, but that woman who tried to get you busted has a son in my little brother's home room. He told my brother, Josh, that his mom said you were *high* when you ran that light."

Sandi Myles came bouncing up at that moment, her arms full of books. "Hi hotshot," she panted "how's the rib cage feeling?" She poked playfully at Marc's middle, grinning winningly all the time.

"Was there something that you wanted?" Susan snapped, glaring at her.

"As a matter of fact there is," Sandi replied, paying absolutely no attention to the almost tangible hatred emanating from Marc's girlfriend. "Marc, can I talk to you right after American Government class? It'll only take a minute."

Marc, confused and angry with himself, took it out on Susan. He gave her a superior look as she slipped into her classroom. "Sure, Sandi." he replied. Then speaking loudly enough to be sure Susan heard, he ended with, "I'd really like to talk to *you, anytime!*"

Sandi squeezed his elbow and they took the stairs two at a time as the bell began ringing. "Gee Sandi, I'm going to be late to class. Old Adams is mad at me already." They were lingering by Sandi's classroom door.

"Forget him Marc," Sandi breathed. She was standing very close and her perfume was almost overpowering. Marc looked around wildly, expecting to see Bob Marsh at any moment. Bob had been Sandi's steady boyfriend for the last three years. He was a weight lifter, and as a junior had gone all the way to the state wrestling finals.

"Are you taking Susan to the Homecoming Dance?" Sandi paid no attention as her speech/drama teacher pointedly closed the classroom door. One more "admit late-unexcused" slip was no concern to her!

"I guess so, we hadn't talked about it. Susan probably wants to go."

"How would you like to take me?" Sandi asked boldly, her huge blue eyes looking up at him coyly. "You know this is the only dance where the girls get to ask the guys!" "Wow! I mean great," Marc sputtered, "but what about Bob?"

"Bob won't be here. He's visiting up at Central State all that weekend. He thinks they're going to offer him a wrestling scholarship."

Marc chewed his lip as he stared down at this beautiful girl. "But what would I tell Susan?" he mumbled.

"Tell her you're going with me!" Sandi declared, hands on her hips. "She doesn't *own* you does she?"

"O.K. Sandi, I'll see you at the dance just as soon as I can get away after the game. But tell me something will you? Why me? I never knew you were interested."

"Come on Marc. It just makes sense. I'm head basketball cheerleader and you're the star ball player. We really should be getting to know each other, you know?"

"I'm not a star," Marc mumbled as they started off towards the office together.

Miss Carlton, the principal's secretary, eyed the couple curiously as she wrote out their admit to class passes. She checked "unexcused" without bothering to ask why they were late. She had heard every possible excuse too many times already!

***

Marc steered his parents' station wagon carefully through the slush as he eased into the student parking lot. Only a little after six and already it was getting dark. He let the engine idle and kept the heater on high. He stared blankly at the brick wall ahead of him, letting the flowing heat bake his feet and legs. His own car was still smashed up. While it could be driven, he was ashamed of the way it looked. Also he felt it reminded everyone of his accident.

Fans were already lining up at the main gym door. These were the ones unlucky enough not to have a season pass. They had to get to the games early in order to find a good seat in the unreserved section. Marc eyed them from the warmth of the wagon. Here was certain proof that winning teams brought out the fans!

Reluctantly he crawled out into the cold and headed for the locker room. The door was locked again! He pounded on it impatiently, then gave it a tremendous shot with his gym bag. The door opened a crack. A burst of warm air flowed into the night.

"We don't want any!" Punchy Markles squeaked in a high, falsetto voice, He slammed the door shut again.

"Come on you clown!" Marc growled, kicking at the door. His gym bag was heavy and he was also trying to keep his clothes for the dance from slipping off their hangers.

"What's the password?" The door opened an inch then closed again. Much laughter could be heard inside.

Marc rammed his shoulder against the door to force his way in. Naturally, Punchy was waiting for this and at the last instant, jumped clear. Everyone clapped and hooted as Marc came hurtling into the room, his gym bag flying! Assistant Coach Jamison laughed as hard as anyone. Coach Crites had not yet arrived. Marc, red faced, felt a sudden, uncontrollable rage. He whirled on Markles, slamming him up against the lockers. The team stared at them in shock. It was only a JOKE!

The reserve team was suiting up. Their warm-up would start in a few minutes. Coach Jamison was moving among them giving last minute instructions and trying to fire them up. Their win-loss record so far was not bad, but a far cry from that of the undefeated varsity. Even as he talked to his boys he kept one eye on Marc.

Marc put his equipment in his locker, carefully hung up his jacket and slacks, and checked his cleaned and pressed uniform. He followed Punchy and the others up the stairs into the gym. The main doors were opened now and the spectators were rapidly filling the stands. Homecoming was always a big event at Paxton. There would be standing room only for the evening.

The student body had voted for homecoming king and queen earlier in the week. To no one's surprise Biggy Nelson had been an almost unanimous choice for king. It had been a real contest for queen, however. When the last ballots were counted it was Sharrit Williams, a cute black cheerleader, over blond and beautiful Sandi Myles by a mere seven votes. Biggy and Sharrit would be crowned during halftime of the reserve contest. The ceremony had become traditional at Paxton over the years.

Nelson was embarrassed by the attention. Sharrit was amazed but elated. Sandi Myles was furious!

As the buzzer ended the first half of the preliminary game a red carpet was unrolled to the center circle. Two chairs, decorated to represent thrones, were hustled into place as the pep band began attempting a solemn march. Biggy, trying to look dignified, came marching down the carpet. His royal robe was far too small and kept slipping off his huge shoulders. By the time he reached his *throne* it looked a lot like Superman's cape!

Sharrit was wearing the traditional queenly robe and train over her cheerleading outfit. Her shining black curls reached just below Biggy's elbow.

The crowning took place with much ceremony in the center circle. The crowd applauded and cheered as each candidate dropped to one knee and received the crown. Everyone tried not to notice how ridiculous Biggy's too small crown looked perched high on his black, completely shaved head. In spite of this the big center handled himself with surprising grace, offering Sharrit his arm and escorting her back to the sideline. They would reign in splendor there until the third quarter when Biggy would have to dress for the varsity game.

Sandi was chewing her gum viciously. The other cheerleaders were staying clear of her, knowing that anything they might say would only anger her more.

The gossip mills at Paxton had been working all week and most of the girls had heard that Sandi had asked Marcus Cassell to be her escort at the homecoming dance. Some thought that what they considered her betrayal of her absent steady boyfriend had been the main reason she was not elected queen.

Sandi continued to sulk, and refused to go out on the floor when the other cheerleaders made up an *honor guard* around the royal thrones. She had not been seen to smile once during the ceremony!

***

Having slipped away from the reserve game near the middle of the third quarter Marc was all alone in the Pacer Pad. It was time to chew one of his leaves. The varsity game would start in a little over half an hour.

Marc gasped as he stared into his open locker. Everything was gone! His sports coat and dress pants for the dance were missing, his good shoes, everything! What horrified him most of all however was his varsity jacket. It was gone too, and in the zipper pocket was his precious malo hierba leaf! Frantically he ripped locker after locker open. He looked behind jackets, shirts, and suits but his thick blue and white Paxton coat was not to be seen.

"I'll get you for this Punchy!" he growled through clenched teeth as he kicked the last locker door closed. In desperation he circled through the assistant coach's office and even looked in Jamison's personal closet. Nothing! Coach Crites' office was locked as usual.

There was only one place left to look; the shower area itself. Stepping carefully onto the slippery tile he flicked on the overhead lights. What a sight! Each shower head held one item of his clothing. His sports coat hung from one, his tie from another. Each shoe neatly enclosed a nozzle. But there at the far end of the room was what he was so desperately seeking. His hard won blue and white team jacket was hanging neatly in the last stall.

Grabbing handfuls of his clothing, Marc dashed back to his locker and threw them in. Sitting on one of the benches he slipped the precious leaf out of its resting place. The thing was so dry it had crumbled into several small pieces. Marc chewed rapidly as he tasted the remaining lint - encrusted fragments from the bottom of his pocket. At that moment the door slid open and the rest of the Paxton varsity came filing into the room. Marc wiped the sweat from his forehead and let his head fall back against the wall.

"Close! Very close!" he breathed. His words were drowned out by the excited chatter of the team's pre-game jitters.

Getting into his white home game jersey, Marc elbowed Punchy in the ribs. "Cute, Punchy! Thanks a lot buddy!"

Punchy was the picture of innocence. "Hey man, what you jabbing on me for?"

"Never mind," Marc replied, "just don't be surprised when you see your trunks hanging from the front lawn flagpole!" He began taping both ankles. He couldn't remember when he had injured them, but they were both plenty sore.

"You're crazy man," Punchy said trying to hide a grin. "I don't know what you're talking about."

"Uh huh. Tell me about it you weirdo!"

Those who were in on the joke laughed and nudged each other. You never knew what Punchy would do next, but on the basketball court he was pure magic!

The reserves had lost a close contest. They slammed into the Pacer Pad and fell onto the benches, hands hanging. Both Crites and Jamison followed them into the room. Every varsity player was watching their head coach.

Ignoring the crestfallen reserve team, Crites stood in the center of the room, legs apart and clipboard in hand. Turning slowly, he made eye contact with each of his twelve team members. He did not speak. When he was certain that every man was focused on the game he jerked his head toward the door. With a roar, the boys sprang up and dashed up the steps into the packed field house. Homecoming was a big deal!

"Marcus, Marcus, Marcus!" The cheerleaders were at it again as Marc and his teammates started their warm-up drill. White satin uniforms fairly sparkled as they circled their half of the floor. Passes zipped back and forth between two lines of Pacers as they wove their way ever closer to the basket. The pep band was in great form and soon the hometown crowd was clapping and stamping in rhythm. Circling now, twelve white warm-up jackets slithered closer and closer together, moving ever nearer to the hoop. No one had as yet taken one shot at the basket. At the final moment Marc whipped one of his now famous behind-the-back passes to Biggy. Like a rocket he erupted from the center of the closed circle of Pacers. The crowd roared in delight as Nelson whipped the ball down in a spectacular, two handed slam.

Paxton had style.

After the dunk each player glided backward out of the circle until they were once again spread across the floor. The team mascot then threw a basketball to each player and the true shooting warm-up began.

Coach Crites hated his team's warm-up theatrics but there was nothing he could do about it. In a rare moment of weakness before the season, he had suggested that the team elect their own captain and devise their own warm-up routines. Punchy had been elected unanimously (which proved he had voted for himself!) and it was he and Mickey Beeler who had worked out the drill. Crites realized how much the fans loved this display but he also knew such grandstanding only worked when your team was on top! Putting on a show like this could make you look like a fool if your ball club was losing.

"None of this kind of stuff next year!" Crites vowed silently as he watched his boys taking their warm-up shots. He did not notice that Marcus Cassell, who would again be starting at guard, had not yet taken a single shot at the basket.

***

Sandi scowled at Marc resentfully. It had taken her a lot of time to go over the score books and stat sheets to get the exact number of perfect shots Marc had made to date. She had the cheering block primed to start the count and keep it up with every warm-up shot, but so far all he had done was dribble around in little circles. Every so often he would bend and stretch before taking some short hops. Finally he dribbled directly under the basket and dropped in a shot which her little brother could have made.

"Fifty-two! Fifty-two! Fifty-two!" The cheering block had been waiting too, but they had to wait some more. Marc did not shoot the ball again.

Cassell was getting worried. The game was starting and still he had hardly begun to feel the effects of the malo hierba. Only a slight tingling in his legs gave any evidence that the drug was working at all.

Mayfield East had been a basketball powerhouse in past years but had fallen dramatically this season. They had lost every game but their first two, and it soon became clear that their record was not going to improve tonight!

Punchy was having a ball! Mayfield's guards were both slow. Their stiff defensive play was exactly what Markles loved to see. Several inches shorter than any of the other players on either team, he had agility and speed. In addition He was a very accurate outside shooter. Crites had made it very clear to both him and Marc that their basic job was to get the ball in to the forwards and center. If this did not work out, however, Punchy could score from almost anywhere on the floor.

Marc let Punchy take control. He did little more than keep Markles out of trouble and return passes to him. He was waiting on the malo hierba!

With the first quarter well under way Punchy once again stole the ball from the hapless Mayfield guards at mid-court. As he had been taught, Marc sprinted toward the Paxton basket on the fast break. Beeler was close behind. Punchy passed to Marc and crossed behind him and Beeler as they worked the figure 8. Marc drove for the basket and took the lead pass from Beeler. Although in excellent position for a left-handed lay-up, Marc dribbled under the basket and flipped a pass back to Beeler. Mickey was so surprised at this move he nearly bobbled the pass. By the time he finally had the ball the two Mayfield guards had converged on him and effectively tied him up. Punchy and Marc were unable to break the Mayfield guards' return.

With the Paxton team spread all over the floor Mayfield easily took the ball in for another two points.

Crites screamed for a time out. Grabbing Marcus with both hands he raged into his face. "What's WITH you, man?" In one game you shoot the ball from all over and now you don't take the lay-up. Stupid, buddy, stupid!"

Marc didn't answer. He hadn't taken the shot because he was certain that the leaf hadn't taken full effect yet. He didn't want to miss and spoil his perfect record. Sandi Myles was watching and, he suspected, so was the news media!

"Sit down and think about it Cassell!" Crites snarled, stabbing one finger at the bench. "You'd better get your head on straight boy, or so help me you won't be playing for me!" He jerked his head at Klear. Surprised, the sub eagerly jumped up and trotted to the scorers' table to report in. Crites gave hasty instructions for the rest of the team and shoved them back onto the court.

Play resumed.

Raymond Klear, Marc's replacement, was having a good night. The ineffective and almost lethargic guards opposing him and

Punchy were no problem. Klear scored several times and by halftime was credited with four excellent assists.

Sandi sulked along the sidelines, shooting accusing glances at Marc from time to time. She went out on the cheering routines with the rest of the girls but anyone could tell she was far from her usual bouncy self.

"You might know," she thought to herself. "I ask this *nerd* to be my date at tonight's dance and he doesn't even get to play!" She had had a secret hope that the WPAX-TV crew might show up after the game. It would be only natural for her to be hanging onto Marc's arm when the cameras started rolling. Who knew? They might even have put the camera on her for awhile. "After all," she told herself, "I am head cheerleader around this dump!" She folded her arms and sent hate stares at the lanky blond guard smiling away on the Paxton bench.

Toward the end of the third quarter Coach Crites began substituting. Once again the Paxton Pacers found themselves holding a comfortable lead. Crites liked to keep his back-up players alert and involved. By using as many substitutes as possible in easy win contests like this one he was also able to maintain bench strength for those times when they were needed.

As each first stringer came out of the game the Paxton rooters cheered and applauded. The fans loved this bunch of winners, and their enthusiasm was growing with every victory.

Raymond Klear rarely got to see much real action, so Crites left him in the game. He was playing a great game. Biggy Nelson stayed in too, of course, but it was not his night. Mayfield East was keying on him and kept him tied up and out of position much of the time. The big center was clearly in charge on defense however, hauling down rebound after rebound, which allowed very few follow-ups after Mayfield's misses.

Crites continued to clear his bench. Finally he was ready to give the Never-Miss-Kid a second chance. He looked down at Marc, who was sitting in his usual spot at the other end, as far from his coach as he could get.

Instant rage! Marc was sitting there grinning like a fool. He was bouncing up and down on the bench like a jack-in-the-box. His hands were slapping his knees, apparently in rhythm with some inner music he was hearing.

"No way!" Crites said aloud. "NO WAY!"

Once again a game ended with Marcus Cassell, the "Never-Miss-Kid," not being able to return to the game. Paxton had chalked up its thirteenth victory, still without a loss. Biggy had (for him) a poor night offensively. His twenty-six points against Mayfield would drop him to fifth place in the Tri-Lakes League individual scoring race.

A small, nattily dressed man rose from his seat on the top row. He crumpled his game program in both hands then threw it into the aisle. He stalked out of the gym.

***

"Hi ya Sweet Thing!" Marcus yelled as he bounded up the locker room steps. "Ready for the big dance?"

"What took you so long?" Sandi asked sullenly. She eyed his still wet blond hair. "I guess you needed a real long shower after all the sweating you did in the game!"

Instead of being hurt or insulted at the cutting remark, Cassell began to giggle! In fact his laughter was so loud and prolonged that the large group of fans waiting by the locker room turned to stare curiously at Cassell. Jumping up and down a little Marc tossed his gym bag into the first row of seats and grabbed Sandi. "Here we go Sandi gal," he yelled swinging her around in a crazy parody of a dance step.

"Let go of me!" Sandi hissed between clenched teeth. It took a lot to embarrass Sandi Myles, but Marc was getting it done!

"O.K., O.K. Let's go! My car's right by the door," Marc stated, grabbing up his gym bag Sandi was so glad to be moving away from the crowd, many of whom were still watching Cassell. They weren't laughing.

The homecoming dance was set up in the junior high across town. Marc drove fast and dangerously, but they made it there.

The music was loud. Very loud. The kids were having a great time. Paxton's winning season made everyone feel good. Even the chaperones were dancing.

Sandi was surprised as she danced with Marc. It seemed that by slightly after eleven o'clock, he seemed to be slowing down by the minute. The dance was not nearly over before he was wanting to sit out about every other dance. His collar was wet with sweat and beads of it were appearing at his hairline. Several times he stumbled a little when first rising from the chairs placed around the walls of the gym.

"Uh, Sandi. I mean uh. well ..." Marc was having trouble making sense. "Do you think you could. uh. well. find somebody to take you home? I uh. uh. don't feel good. Well I really I feel awful! I think I'm sick."

"Great! Just GREAT!" Sandi snapped. She folded her arms and stared straight ahead. "Some basketball star! I ask you to take me and it's hardly started and you want to ditch me already!"

"I'm. I'm sorry Sandy. Really, really sorry, but I just can't, can't." Marc held his head with both hands.

"Go on then. Just go on! I'll catch a ride with Marci and Ted. I'm going to call my boyfriend when I get home, even if it is long distance."

"Aw Sandi... uh don't be mad. I ..."

"Shut up! Just shut up! You make me sick!"

"I'm sick alright," Marc mumbled as Sandi flounced away.

Standing on the sidelines, Marcus was wondering what had happened during the game. He knew they had won, but nobody was talking to him about it. It seemed that the other players were sort of avoiding him. He felt terrible, and most of all it was nausea. These memory losses were really starting to worry him.

"Marc! Hey Marc!" Mrs. Slater, who had been one of his junior high teachers, had to shout to be heard above the booming rock music. "Come with me, I've got to talk to you a minute."

Marc stumbled along after her. He had already forgotten Sandi Myles.

In the much quieter lobby the teacher put one hand on Marc's arm and looked closely at him for a moment. Marc was surprised. She wasn't the kind who usually got so close.

"You look terrible! Are you sick? Do you feel like you're going to faint? Here," she urged, "you'd better sit down a minute."

Standing over him, she hesitated only slightly then began. "I'm afraid I have some bad news. The phone was ringing in the office so I answered it. It was your mother. She was calling from City General over in Springfield. Your dad has been taken to the hospital."

Marc looked shocked. "What's he doing over in Springfield? He always goes to the hospital here."

"Marc, I'm afraid this is very serious. He's in intensive care. They're saying he's critical. Your mother wants you to come as soon as you can."

A tear slid down the side of Marc's nose. Angrily he wiped it off. He didn't speak.

"I can see you're not in any shape to drive all the way to Springfield this late by yourself," she said.

"I can do it," Marc mumbled.

"You won't need to," Mrs. Slater replied. "I talked to Mr. Jamison before I talked to you. He insisted on taking you himself."

"Well what about Sandi?" Marc asked. He had forgotten that she had already told him she would find her own way home.

Coach Jamison and his wife came hurrying up, their faces twisted with concern. He dropped an arm around Marc's shoulders and hung on. To Marc it felt as if an anvil had been placed on his back.

CHAPTER EIGHT

Tuesday afternoon's practice went well. Crites was happy with the team, or at least about as happy as he ever became. The Pacers were still leading the league, and were the only unbeaten team. Also, the booster club meeting had been a hot one on Monday, but Crites had come out on top. No one had hassled him about benching Marcus Cassell. In fact most of the club members could see that Crites was right in his handling of the unpredictable "Never-Miss-Kid." The coach actually smiled a little as he checked the locker room and turned out the lights.

Assistant Coach Jamison followed Crites out of the darkened gym. He hunched his head deeper into his collar against that falling snow and trotted towards his car. He started the engine and waited for Crites to pull away from the parking lot. As the wipers scrabbled at the frozen slush he noticed a figure standing under the overhang by the main gym doors. It was Cassell. Swinging his car around toward the entrance, he opened his window and yelled. "You got a ride, Marc?"

"Waiting on my mom," Marc yelled trying not to shiver. He had pulled his stocking cap down over his ears and had both hands jammed into his jacket pockets.

"Get in here," Jamison yelled, leaning across to unlock the door on the passenger side.

Marc slapped at his blue jeans to knock off the snow as he crawled into the car. "Thanks Coach," he said gratefully. He was still shivering a little.

"Why didn't you stay inside till your mother got here? The janitor would have locked up after you."

"Mom was supposed to be here by now. She went to Springfield to see Dad in the hospital, so she needed the wagon. I can't. that is uh. my car isn't fixed yet."

"Want me to run you home?" Jamison asked turning the heater up a notch.

"Better not, Mom should be coming pretty soon now."

"How's your dad doing by now? Is he still in intensive care?"

"Aaron Jamison watched the wipers licking the last of the snow from the windshield. He did not look at Marc, knowing how serious the boy's father's condition had become.

"He's about the same I guess," Marc answered, fiddling with the gym bag he was holding on his lap. "We'll probably know more after mom gets the results of the tests he had today." Neither man spoke for a few minutes. The engine idled softly, the sound muffled by several inches of snow on the hood.

"Hey Marc," Jamison began hesitantly, "I've been wanting to talk to you for a while about. well you know, how things have been going." Marc did not reply.

"I mean you've got great moves! I've seen you do things on that court that I can hardly believe. Then other times. I don't know. it looks like. well like you don't care about us coaches. Or anybody else for that matter. Sometimes you act kind of goofy during the games. I don't see that in practice."

Cassell remained silent. He stared fixedly at the entrance to the parking lot, willing the old green station wagon to appear.

Having started this, Coach Jamison went doggedly on. "You've been playing for us for four years now. You know what Crites is like. Maybe you think it's personal, but it isn't. He's a stickler on discipline. The guy demands cooperation from every player on the ball club. It wouldn't matter if it was you or Beeler or even Nelson. Anybody who doesn't follow his game plan is going to get it. Right?"

"Yeah, I know coach, but ..."

Jamison waited for Marc to continue but the boy did not do so. The coach probed a little deeper. "Marc," he began a little hesitantly, "is there anything you want to tell me? We're all alone here and anything we talk about won't have to go any further. You have my word on it."

For the first time, Marc turned and looked directly at Jamison. The coach thought the kid was going to speak but after a moment

Marc turned away and again peered desperately toward the parking lot entrance.

"Look Marc, I've got kids of my own. You know that. Jerry's almost twelve. Believe me I want to help you if I can. And not just for the team's sake either."

"I know it coach," Marc murmured staring down at his hands.

"This is getting nowhere," Jamison thought. Hoping that Mrs. Cassell would not arrive for a few minutes yet, he decided to come directly to the point. "Cassell, I want to ask you something. I swear to you that whatever you tell me will go no further than the two of us. Okay?"

Marc glanced warily at the coach then looked away again. He gave no answer.

"Remember the Kirtland game? I know I'll never forget it!" Jamison was shaking his head at the memory. "Almost a riot, Biggy kicked out Coach Crites ejected from the game! Wow! You know I sort of let you loose in that one and you really went wild! I never saw anyone play like that."

"That was some night alright!" Marc grinned taking his eyes off the parking lot. "We were lucky to win it."

"It was more than luck, Cassell. You pulled it off for us like a one man army! Some people though are beginning to think things and say things."

Marc was sitting very still. No part of his body moved.

Jamison swung himself around until he was facing Cassell. "Have you been experimenting with any kind of uh. medication? Like drugs or maybe steroids?"

"There's Mom! Thanks Coach!" Marc slipped and nearly fell as he leaped from the car and sprinted through the falling snow toward the big car pulling cautiously onto the lot.

Jamison shook his head in frustration as he backed slowly away from the school. The snow was already beginning to fill his tire tracks as he pulled into the street. "Well I tried," he said aloud. The words came out as one long sigh. "Thank Heaven for Christmas vacation," he thought. All of them, coaches and players alike needed some time off.

Crites had surprised everybody (and angered quite a few) by refusing to enter the Pacers in the traditional Holiday Invitational tournament. He had never liked these contests during the winter break, but was bullied into entering by the Boosters' Club. Riding on a thirteen game winning streak, the coach felt secure enough to say no and make it stick.

"What have you got against a couple of games over vacation?" One booster had growled in a previous meeting.

"Because," Crites had bristled, "in the first place it doesn't mean anything! Wins and losses don't count against a team's record, scoring isn't figured in. None of that. In the second place, I haven't said this publicly, and I won't, but I've got a *feeling!* This could be the year for Paxton. I'm talking about a chance of going all the way to State!"

"But wouldn't a couple more games be good experience for our guys?"

Another booster took up the cause. "I think we could win it easy this year. A nice new trophy ought to fire up the team for the rest of the season wouldn't it?"

With a true effort Crites kept his voice even as he replied. "Well we're practically taping Cassell together now. Nelson and Beeler both have ankle problems. I don't want to get any one of my boys hurt in some silly, meaningless tournament game and have them out of action for the rest of the season. And as for experience, well they'll get plenty of that in practice over the holidays. We'll be going two-a-day some of the time, but with no holiday tournament they'll have several days completely off."

The Paxton administration had backed the coach on his decision, so there was little the Boosters could do about it. They weren't happy, but most had to admit that Crites' reasons made sense. The possibility of the Pacers going to the State tournament did a lot to ease their pain.

***

The vacation had flown by. Before they knew it the date was January fifth.

Wellington, scheduled for the coming Friday night, promised to be another real test for the Pacers. While only in third place in the league, this fast and well-coached team was coming on. They had won six of their last seven starts, with the latest victories showing very lopsided scores.

Crites had been bullying his team unmercifully all week, trying his best to beat into them his plan for stopping Wellington's murderous *run and gun* style of play. Scouting reports on them all stressed the same thing; if allowed to get the rebound they were away and gone!

"Man coach, I've had it!" Punchy gasped, having just chased down another full court fast break.

"Two laps Markles!" Crites snapped, grabbing the ball from Punchy's sweating hands. The exhausted guard trotted off to take his punishment, muttering to himself. Crites ignored him and pulled up a sub in his place. Marc Cassell, playing with the varsity once again, was nearly out of it too, but he forced himself to keep going, knowing he was still on very shaky ground with the coach. How he wished for a malo hierba leaf at that moment. He would show them some fancy defensive work then!

After the long practice session finally ended both first and second stringers dragged themselves off to the showers, hardly speaking.

"Man, I'm glad Wednesday is finally over!" Biggy Nelson drawled. He was sitting on one end of the locker room bench, a towel draped over his head. He was still in his ragged practice jersey. "About one more practice like that and I'm dead meat man!" Nobody said anything. Finally he hauled himself erect and padded off to the showers. Everyone was thinking the same thing; tomorrow was Thursday, that meant a light practice, and probably some time viewing Wellington scouting films. They would live!

***

"Hello Marc," Susan said, her voice giving no indication of her mood. Marc jumped. He hadn't seen her sitting in her car beside his now repaired Mustang.

"Hi Susan, how you doing?"

"I've seen better days. I haven't been sleeping so well lately. Do you want to get in my car for a minute? We need to talk."

"Well your car is sure going to be warmer than mine," Marc answered trying to sound friendly. He set his gym bag on the hood of the Mustang and crawled into her small car. Marc had to let the seat back to accommodate his long legs. He made a big production of it, stalling for time and giving the girl a chance to start it. Susan didn't say anything, however. Both kids sat and stared out of the windshield watching an occasional snowflake melt against the warming glass.

Marc finally plunged in. "I'm uh. sorry about the other night," he said, still not looking to his left.

"Oh? What night was that?" Susan queried haughtily.

"You know, the homecoming dance last Friday night."

"Oh that's right! I remember now. Funny I haven't seen you or talked to you since then I guess." Susan's voice caught and she was unable to continue.

"Come on Sue," Marc grumped, "you can quit acting so smart any time. Anyway she asked me you know! I hadn't heard any invitation from you before that either!"

"You CREEP!" Susan wailed, "You knew perfectly well I was going to. Why don't you just get out of the car and leave me alone. Go see your snippy little cheerleader again!"

Marc whirled to face her. He was about to make an equally angry reply when he saw a big tear squeeze out of her right eye and leave a shiny trail down her cheek. That did it. He never could stand to see a girl's tears. "Well I guess I should tell you that you're not the only one mad at me. Sandi hates me too. I didn't even take her home after the dance. I got sick again."

"I know that," Susan said scrubbing viciously at her tears with the back of one hand, "so does everybody else at Paxton too! You made me look like a fool. I'm glad she told you off. You two deserve each other! Now please leave my car."

"Aw come on Susan," Marc pleaded, turning to face her again, "why don't you come over to my house tonight. We can talk more about it then. I said I'm sorry and I am. I guess that's all I can say right now."

Susan glared out of the window for a while, then said, "I just don't know, Marc. Maybe I'll come and then again maybe I won't! Now if you will kindly get out of the car I've got to get going."

Marc dragged himself into the cold, picked up his gym bag and clambered into the frigid Mustang. He watched as Susan sped out of the lot, her car skidding dangerously on the packed snow. He sat there with both hands on the wheel, feeling as if the weight of the world was coming right down on his back. "Well now I guess that makes just about everybody," he thought sadly. "Might as well have them all mad at me I reckon." He pumped the accelerator and coaxed the Mustang into life. It was a long, sad drive home.

***

"What time is it?" Marc yelled.

Mrs. Cassell's answer floated up the stairs. "It's ten past eight. That's exactly five minutes later than the last time you asked! My goodness Marcus, what is the matter with you?"

Marc didn't answer. He slammed his heavy chemistry book shut and pushed it off his bed. It landed with a bang.

"Marc, please!" his mom had climbed the stairs to his room door. "Your father needs his rest now. Between the two of us I'm sure he has been awake all this time. We're lucky they even let me bring him home tonight."

Again Marc made no reply. She waited a few minutes outside his door, then with an exasperated sigh gave up and went back down.

Marc put his stocking feet on the headboard and stared at the ceiling. His father did need his rest. The lab reports had been frank and very grim. Paul Cassell would almost certainly need full time care in a nursing home before very long. "Well that's one more thing I can worry about," Marc thought. He flung one arm over his eyes and tried to concentrate on the music from his stereo.

The front doorbell rang.

Buttoning his shirt, Marc thumped down the stairs without bothering to hunt for his sneakers. Mrs. Cassell was opening the door as he skidded to a stop at the bottom. Susan came in with a smile for Marc's mom. Her coat collar was pulled high around her ears and flecks of snow still glittered on her short brown hair.

"Hi Marc," she said, acting friendly for Meg's benefit, "got your chemistry done?" She tossed her books into an easy chair and started to shrug out of her coat.

"Help her with her coat Marc," his mother clucked, shaking her head. Marc did so, rather awkwardly. Susan plopped down on the sofa as Marc headed back upstairs for his books. They both knew books were only for appearances. They had more important things to discuss than *chemistry!* Meg Cassell was no fool. She knew it too. She left quietly, heading for the dining room where her husband was resting on the daybed they had arranged for him there.

Meg hoped whatever troubles these two had would be over soon. It had been a bad fall and winter; her husband seriously ill, Marc's on again-off again relationship with his team, his wreck and arrest, the strange and frightening spells her son seemed to have after each ball game, and now apparently there was a problem between the boy and his girlfriend. She slumped beside her husband's sleeping form and wished for spring.

CHAPTER NINE

Marc was elated! He had figured it out during the first few minutes of this, his sixth period calculus class. He could not think of a single reason it wouldn't work.

"Oh man, that's it!" he told himself, paying no attention to the complicated mathematical material Mr. Foster was explaining in his usual maddeningly patient style.

"Why didn't I think of this before?" he wondered. His eyes were on the instructor but he was seeing himself at the game which was only a few hours away.

Earlier he had been thinking about his father and the latest test results. Marc's mother had told him privately that his dad was failing rapidly, but that they were doing everything they could for him. She had mentioned that the neurologist had suspected that Paul might be over-medicated, and therefore had suggested reducing the strength of some of his medicine.

"Over MEDICATED!" The words echoed and re-echoed in Marc's brain. *"That's what's wrong!"* he thought again. Tonight rather than chew an entire malo hierba leaf right away, he planned to use only part of one before the game, and sneak the rest of it at half time. It had to work!

Things were looking up at last. He had patched it up with Susan, at least for the present, and with his secret plan for tonight's game he couldn't see how there would be a problem. He didn't realize he was smiling, but Mr. Foster did.

"Do you find my explanation amusing Mr. Cassell?" The instructor's sarcasm alerted the class, several of whom were about as far out of it as Marc was. They turned to stare at their classmate, happy that something was finally happening to liven things up a little.

"No. guess I was thinking of something else."

This brought laughter from the rest of the class. Mr. Foster pushed his glasses higher on his nose and continued to glare at his target. "Perhaps you would like to tell the rest of us just exactly what it was that you were thinking of," he suggested, leaning against the desk. There was a long pause. "Well? It certainly couldn't have been mathematics. That is if your last two test results are any indication!"

"The game tonight I guess, sorry."

Foster frowned at him some more but decided not to badger the boy any further. How he hated the way sports stars were favored at this school! Still, he found himself doing it too. "The game is then, this is now. Pay attention!" The teacher was rather proud of the phrase he had used and of the way he had ended the situation. He went back to his lecture.

***

"Hey man, these meetings are startin' to jive!" Biggy Nelson said aloud. The group laughed. "somebody ask a really good one!" he shouted.

Katie Soren raised a hand. Tall and pretty, Katie had been named first team all-league three years in a row. A senior now, she had been offered several volleyball scholarships. Usually quiet and rather shy (except on the volleyball court!) the group was surprised that she would volunteer.

"I read the Bible quite a bit," she began, "and I go to Bible study some of the time when volleyball is over. I can get what most of it means, but sometimes I'm confused. Why doesn't God come right out and tell us what to do and how to act?"

Janet Compton had been unable to attend so the vice-chairman, sophomore Mel Solon, was in charge. He surprised everyone by taking the question himself, rather than defer it to Coach Jamison.

"Listen Katie, even though you won't go out with me, I'll tell you what I think will help."

"You're too short," she yelled. Everyone laughed.

"A couple years ago," Mel continued (not in the least offended since he *was* pretty short) "I read a thing in one of Mom's books. I never forgot it. There was this little girl, I guess she was about three or so, who needed some kind of blood transfusions every couple of days. She hated them, 'cause they hurt a lot. But she had to have them to get better. Her dad and mom did everything they could think of to get her through the shots and IV's and stuff, but she still cried and screamed as soon as they got near the hospital. The three of them got through it somehow, and I guess the little girl got O.K. The point is that the parents could have set her down and explained about the transfusions, white blood counts, and all that. But would that have done any good?"

Mel waited for a few minutes but nobody volunteered anything.

"Well?" he demanded.

Still nothing.

"You jerks!" he yelled. "All that little girl knew was the shots hurt. The way I figure it, Katie, it's the same with God. If He explained everything in His plan for us we wouldn't understand it anyway. God is smarter than us!"

To Mel's astonishment the group gave him a round of applause. Only a few good-natured boos were heard.

Coach Aaron Jamison said a brief prayer of thanks for his involvement with this group. He was surprised and gratified that the club members were assuming more and more of the leadership.

***

The gym was overflowing with noisy bodies. Wellington had almost as great a following as Paxton. Fans had started arriving well before game time, anticipating a real scrap between the league leaders.

Marc sat with his teammates in the players' section under the south basket. The reserve game was under way, but the crowd was not enthused. The Pacers were taking a beating from the much larger and faster Wellington five.

THE KID WHO COULDN'T MISS

For the third time in a half hour Marc eased the pack of gum out of his shirt pocket. He felt pretty clever Earlier that evening he had very carefully broken one of the dry malo hierba leaves into two nearly equal pieces, He had then unwrapped two sticks of gum, inserted the leaves, and wrapped each piece up again. He checked his watch, and when it was time, opened one of the little packets and popped the contents into his mouth. He had chosen a moment when there was a scramble on the ball court and everyone's attention was on the game. He was pretty sure no one had noticed.

Marc had been happy and a little surprised to see his name posted as a starter in tonight's game. He didn't know that the assistant had talked with Crites and convinced him to give Cassell another chance. "I had a talk with Marc the other night," Jamison had told Crites, "and I really think he'll do what's right now if you let him have a shot at it." The head coach had agreed, thinking it might also keep some of the booster club members from getting on him again about Cassell. And if the kid started messing up he could always bench him. He no longer worried about the Boosters, as he sensed that they were beginning to wonder about the Never-Miss-Kid too.

The Paxton reserve team slunk off the floor to the showers, the scoreboard still broadcasting their shame. They had gone down big, 68-39, but the game to follow was what everyone had come to see. They would not be disappointed.

Marc took only the easiest shots during the warm-up. The malo hierba was working, there was no doubt of that, but he didn't want to risk a miss, even before the game. He was not surprised that neither the cheerleaders nor the cheering block had done any chanting or counting his hits. They were all aware of his shaky status on the team and most figured his amazing record was only a fluke anyway. Marc was glad. He had enough people watching him already.

With four minutes of warm-up time still to go Coach Crites called the team over for his final instructions. He was determined to stop Wellington's fast break, a fact the team was more than aware of, having been screamed at and run hard all week.

"You know what to do," Crites growled, looking directly at Marc. "We've worked on this all week. Everybody does his job. Nobody tries to play it alone. We can beat this bunch, but you've got to follow the plan. You remember what happened three years ago don't you?" They all nodded. Wellington had humiliated a young Pacer team 102-76. "All right let's do it!"

As the Pacers took the floor, Crites grabbed Marc by the shirt and pulled him close. His words were lost in the noise of the gym to all but Marc. "Here's your chance kid. Don't blow it!"

Marc fought down the urge to jump up and down a couple of times as the referee lined them up for the tip-off. With only half as much of the drug's effect he felt wonderful, but more in control. He could even remember the Coach's last words to him. So far his new *half a leaf plan* was working!

Wellington showed their stuff early. Biggy Nelson had taken the tip, but a green-shirted player snatched it away and a three man fast break took it down for a score. It had taken four seconds. Punchy and Marc brought the ball back and worked it in to the forwards. Beeler missed a jumper in the lane. Wellington had Nelson and Brian Kelly blocked out of position. They snatched the rebound and whipped the ball out to the side where their guard was waiting. Immediately the machine went into motion again. The green shirts were a blur as they tore down court. Very little dribbling was needed, as their passes were fast and accurate. Punchy and Marc fell back and crossed lanes as their coach had drilled them, but Brian Kelley, the forward, was unable to get back fast enough. With the three on two the lay-up was easy and with only twenty seconds gone the score was four-zip!

Crites didn't wait. He signaled to Punchy for a time out as the Wellington fans screamed and hooted. They were loving it!

"Slow it down," he barked as the Pacers crowded in close, "Kelley, you're going to have to stay out with the guards more. Cassell, I want. you to go man-to-man on their Willie Taylor. He's number 38. Don't be afraid to use a little contact! If we can stop him we can interrupt their break. Got it?" Marc didn't need Taylor's number. He had been reading about him in the papers all season!

The Pacers slapped hands and trotted onto the court. Punchy passed in to Marc and they moved the ball toward the defense.

Dribbling and passing steadily and with deliberation they worked the ball around the perimeter. Biggy and Beeler drifted back and forth across the lane, waiting for the pass. Play had slowed considerably. Marc concentrated hard on what he thought the coach had told him. The words came through slowly, as through a fog of mist. It took all his will power, but by repeating the words over and over to himself he was able to recall his coach's instructions.

Biggy's arm went up as he slid into position for his favorite shot. Marc lofted the ball high over the defenders exactly into Nelson's hand. The big man took it up and laid it gently against the backboard. It dropped through for the score as the Paxton rooters came alive.

Marc danced through the defense and shadowed his man. He felt as if he knew Willie Taylor personally. Coach Crites had ended every practice by showing the scouting tapes of various Wellington East's games. Number thirty eight had been a standout in nearly every contest. His muscular upper body and heavy legs made him look more like a football player than a basketball guard, but in this case looks certainly were deceiving!

In a slight crouch, Cassell stuck to his man, hands up and arms extended. Whenever the Wellington player had the ball Marc would guard him even closer, letting an arm brush his chest or pushing a knee into Taylor's shin. The strategy helped, as the green shirts were forced to slow their game a little too. Despite the Pacers' furious defensive play, however, Wellington scored again. With two minutes gone the score was eight to two.

Marcus Cassell went into action!

The effect of the malo hierba was in full force. Marc was grinning a little as he and Punchy flipped the ball back and forth, bringing the action up against the Wellington front line. Taking a short pass from Beeler, Marc stopped dead and dribbled easily. Beeler broke toward the basket, trying to get open. Two Wellington players dropped back with him, opening the narrow passage Marcus was waiting for. He slipped into the hole and went up for the jumper the ball sailed straight and true into the basket, but Marc was already zipping to the opposite sideline to intercept Willie Taylor. The scoreboard had hardly blinked Paxton's new tally until Marc was worrying the burly Wellington guard.

Marc danced and flagged both arms at Willie, who was trying to pass the ball in bounds after the score. Punchy was dogging the other guard as the clock ticked on. Finally seeing one of his forwards dropping back to help, the harried Wellington star tried a long pass up court. Mickey Beeler slipped in front of his man and intercepted. He bounce-passed around a green shirted guard to Punchy who whipped it across court to a grinning Marcus Cassell. He took two dribbles, scooped the ball high above Willie Taylor's fingers and layed it in.

Crites' gum was taking awful punishment as he forced himself to stay seated on the bench. He was especially eyeing Cassell, watching for any indication of what might be considered irresponsible playing. So far he could see nothing to complain about.

Once again Wellington brought the ball toward the Paxton basket. Having been forced to slow the game down, they appeared nervous and less confident. Marc continued to worry number thirty-eight, using just enough contact to shake him up, but still avoid being called for the foul. Willie Taylor was irritated but too experienced a player to let the close guarding affect his style. By dribbling almost behind his body, he was able to protect the ball and still continue to set up the plays Wellington liked to use.

Marc watched his man almost with admiration. It was unusual to see a player of Taylor's size handle himself with such finesse. Cassell soon learned to anticipate what his opponent was going to do with the ball. He noticed that whenever the Wellington guard pulled his left foot back a little he was preparing to bring the ball around to the front and pass it away. Marc grinned happily and stayed on his man. It happened again! The left foot was sliding back. The malo hierba slowed everything down nicely, making it easy for Marc to anticipate the series of smooth, controlled actions which had always served Willie Taylor so well. As the ball dropped toward the floor, the Wellington guard started his move. Marc's left hand flicked in and hooked the ball away, barely grazing a muscular thigh. A big smile split his face, but as he dribbled the ball away the rear court referee whistled him back on a called foul.

Wellington made the foul, then surprised the Pacers by what was evidently a pre-arranged, sudden full court press. Paxton, unable to adjust, lost the ball and the green shirts scored again. With the score now eleven to six Coach Crites again signaled for Markles to call a time out.

"Nelson, you and Beeler have to get it together out there," he bristled, a fistful of jersey in each hand, "Look back before you drop back on defense! Help those guards and you can break that press. We worked on that the whole Tuesday practice. THINK! He shoved them back on the floor.

Glancing at the scoreboards as he dribbled deliberately across the mid-court line, Marc decided it was time to take charge. The narcotic contained in the half leaf he had chewed before the game was dancing through his veins. This made it difficult, but he was able to keep from running wild as he had done in previous contests. The best thing was that by now he could remember much of what Crites had told them. He rocketed a pass to Punchy, faked his own guard out of position and took a return flip at the top of the key. He went up gently, the ball cradled in both hands until he was off the floor. His right hand brought the ball high and sent it floating easily off on its unerring course to the hoop. Paxton fans cheered as the three pointer dropped through.

Wellington came back up court after the score, number thirty-eight once again using his behind-the-body dribble as he prepared to set one of their well-drilled plays into motion. Marc was all over him, ready to snag the ball again, when the whistle blew. Another foul on Cassell. The referees were watching Marc and had evidently decided to call him on some of the more obvious bodily contact situations. Marc just smiled away, seemingly in full agreement with the call. The Paxton fans, not so charitable, roared their disapproval.

Willie Taylor held one of the best foul shooting percentages in the league but he missed this one. Unfortunately for the blue and white clad Pacers, the Wellington center went up for the rebound and tipped it in.

Marc and Punchy worked the ball out front until Marc suddenly started a drive directly toward one Wellington forward. Another green shirt converged on him and it appeared certain that Cassell would be tied up. He suddenly sprang straight up, high above his defenders.

At the apex of his leap he fired the ball hard to Mickey Beeler who was open underneath. He banked it in for two, then thrilled the fans by intercepting Wellington's in-bound pass. He looped the ball to Marc, who was still twenty feet out. Without hesitation Marcus banked it in for another three points.

Wellington called time out. The score was tied at nineteen with the first quarter nearly half gone.

The game went on. Paxton was managing to hang on to a slight lead, but Wellington threatened constantly. Marcus Cassell was brilliant. He had scored seven field goals, and two free throws still without a miss. But he had also collected another personal foul.

As the first half ended the Paxton fans leaped from their seats to give the entire Pacer team a standing ovation.

In the locker room Coach Crites was talking so loudly and so fast he was spitting all over Russell Klear who was seated closest to the chalkboard. Cassell eased himself off the bench and fumbled with the team jacket he had purposely left lying on the floor near his locker.

"You listening Cassell?" Crites boomed, glaring at the guard who had caused him so much trouble.

"Sorry coach, getting some gum," Marc answered shakily. He quickly palmed the special stick of "gum" and dropped to his place on the bench. The coach went on, chips of chalk flying as he outlined the defensive changes he wanted for the second half.

Marc teased the wrapper off as quietly as possible. He watched for a good chance to pop the folded half leaf into his mouth. It was then he discovered a problem. Someone had evidently stepped on or kicked his jacket. The malo hierba was a mass of crumbs!

Thinking fast, Marc suddenly pretended to develop a terrible coughing fit. As expected, Crites glared at him and pointed to the fountain, having never stopped his strategy tirade. Continuing to cough and strangle, Marc hurried to the fountain. With his back to the team he quickly dumped the leaf fragments into his palm. He licked them up while pretending to get a drink. Although red-faced and sweating from near discovery, he looked no different from the rest of the players who had been part of the fast and furious action of the first half.

Marc's knee was swelling a little. How had that happened? The trainer taped it up. Nelson jostled Marcus as they ran up the stairs into the gym. "You on something man?" he whispered hoarsely, punching Marc in the ribs.

"What do you mean?" Marc asked, alarmed.

"Hey I seen you man. You been gobbling up something before the game and just now. I ain't no fool! I been seeing all the signs."

"Listen Biggy," Marc whispered desperately, "I've got to talk to you. Maybe after the game tonight, OK?"

The buzzer brought them back to the floor before Nelson could reply. Marc chewed fast, shoving tiny bits of vegetation around with his tongue. He could tell the half leaf he had taken earlier was rapidly wearing off. It would be a few minutes before the new amount would take effect. The solution was easy. He knew exactly what he had to do.

The first time Willie Taylor had the ball Marc made a purposely clumsy grab for the ball. The two came together as the ball squirted into the stands. Both referees' whistles were screaming. Marc had just picked up his fourth personal foul.

As expected, Crites sent Russell Klear in for Cassell. "No problem Marc," the coach said as the boy, pretending disgust, dropped into his familiar spot at the end of the bench. Marc was a little surprised that the coach hadn't given him a hard time about committing his fourth personal foul, but it didn't matter. Safely out of the contest for at least a few minutes, the malo hierba would soon be doing its job!

Early in the fourth quarter, Marcus Cassell was again on the playing floor. By now most of the spectators had become used to the goofy grin the kid always seemed to have. It seemed to the fans that they had never seen a high school player having more fun on the court. Not only was he enjoying himself immensely, he was playing astonishing basketball! Firing almost dangerously long jumpers, most of them from well beyond the three point circle, he continued to score. He did not miss!

The video cameras were rolling. More and more, the huge zoom lenses snaked out and zeroed in on blue jersey number forty-four. The W-PAX TV crew was finally getting the necessary footage for a serious piece on the amazing Paxton player who was once again being called the Never-Miss-Kid The only problem was, would anyone from beyond the Tri-Lakes League ever believe them?

The Paxton Pacers won going away, the final score reading eighty-six to eighty. In spite of having sat out nearly all of the third quarter, Marc had scored thirty-eight, made eleven confirmed assists, and on defense had held Wellington's star player to a mere fourteen points.

CHAPTER TEN

"Come on man hurry up! My girlfriend's over there making mean faces at me already!" Biggy kept one big hand on the door handle as he spoke.

The outside security lights painted Marc's stocking cap as he tried to think how to begin.

"Well Nelson," he began, "It's a long story and you probably won't believe it."

"Marcus, Marcus, move your mouth son! I've got to get going. My guess is you're into some kind of junk, right?"

Marc was fighting the rising nausea which he now expected after every game. "Well in a way I guess I am. But I'm not hooked on anything."

"That's what they all say, baby! Now you just tell old Bi Daddy here what I can do to help you out. Whatever it is, it ain't as bad as it seems!"

"This is going to sound crazy," Marc began, "but I swear to you it's all true!"

"What's true?" It was Susan. Neither of them had seen her come up to Marc's car. Marc whirled around.

"Susan! I thought you already went home."

"I drove myself. She stood on one foot, then the other. Do we have to stand out here ad freeze?"

"O.K. man," Biggy sighed, "we might as well all hear this." He let out a piercing whistle and motioned to his girlfriend to come over. All four squeezed into the Mustang. Marc started the engine and let it idle.

Cassell gripped the top of the steering wheel with both hands and watched the windshield slowly cloud over with steam. "When I was down in Mexico last summer I found these leaves. They call them "malo hierba." I think it means 'bad stuff' or 'no good weed' or something like that."

"Loco weed?" Biggy's girl asked. No one laughed.

Ignoring Celeste, Marc continued. "Well, see I found out that ..."

Bang! Bang! Bang! Someone was pounding on the top of the car!

"What the ...?" Biggy gasped. "What's happening?"

"Come on out Cassell, we need to talk, friend!"

Marc recognized the voice immediately. He had forgotten all about Mr. John Smith and his motorcycle!

"Lock your door!" he whispered to Susan as he snapped the lock on his side. "You in trouble with this dude?" Biggy asked.

"Yeah I am. He had a big bet on that I would miss the first shot in the next game I played in. He was gonna give me a motorcycle if I missed on purpose."

"Get out of the car Cassell! Now!" Smith sounded mean.

"Come on man let's see what this creep is made of," Biggy drawled. He reached up, unlocked Marc's door, and started pushing on the driver's seat with his knees.

Marc's breath was coming fast as he climbed out. Biggy uncoiled himself one leg at a time until he too was standing in the snow. With the car between them the three sized each other up. Mr. Smith stared in shock at the huge black man who literally towered over the car.

"This is between Cassell and me," Smith growled keeping both eyes on Biggy who had started to move around the hood toward him. "We had a little DEAL going. Right Cassell?"

Marc said nothing, but followed the big Paxton center as he sidled toward the gambler.

"Marcus here is my friend," Biggy stated in a kindly tone. "Now you wouldn't want to hassle my FRIEND would you?" He moved closer.

Smith took a step back. "Get out of my face, big guy! Like I said, this is between me and the 'Never-Miss-Kid' here."

Marc moved up beside Nelson and both young men looked down on the small, nervous-looking person. Smith was cautious but not a coward. His eyes darted back and forth between the two ball players, both of whom were watching him carefully. "Back off!" he spat, holding his ground. His right hand moved toward the cleft between the top two buttons of his expensive aviator type jacket. Marc didn't realize the significance of the slowly moving hand but Biggy did.

The big man's right hand shot out like a striking snake. His fingers clamped down hard on the gambler's wrist. "Don't try it man!" He growled, jerking his hand away. Biggy hung onto the man's wrist and slammed him hard against the car. The girls' faces appeared at the windows, their mouths making silent "O's" as they took in the action. Smith scrabbled at his jacket front with his left hand. Before he could reach the gun riding snugly in its holster under Smith's coat, Biggy smashed his left elbow into the man's Adam's apple. Smith tried to twist away but Marc leaped in and grabbed him around the waist.

"Give me the gun, dude!" Biggy grunted, twisting the arm down and in. Smith struggled, his breath coming in short whistles and wheezes.

"Get the gun Marc!" Nelson yelled. He was losing his grip. Marc jabbed one hand inside the man's jacket, but being unfamiliar with shoulder holsters, was unable to get his hand on the weapon. Smith broke loose and ran into the street. When he felt he was safe, he turned and tried to shout a threat. The only sound he could manage was a stage whisper. He appeared to be seriously injured.

Biggy threw one arm over Marc's shoulder as they watched Smith's sports car disappear into the night. Their combined breath hovered over them in a steam cloud as they turned back to the Mustang. They both knew they had not seen the last of the man with the gun! They all left in a hurry.

Cassell had to stop twice on the drive home. He was a very sick person!

***

"Hi Pop," Marc said looking up from his cereal in surprise. His father had not been coming to breakfast for some time.

"I don't like that name and you know it," Paul Cassell whispered, trying to maneuver his wheelchair a little closer to the table. Marc got up and slid the chair sideways enough to allow the wheels to clear the table leg. Mr. Cassell did not thank him.

Paul Cassell was noticeably weaker. Marcus was not surprised at the curt manner his father showed. The man was very sick and probably in pain. Everything that happened was an irritation to him. This was the first time he had been out of bed for a meal in several weeks.

"Sorry Dad. Did you tape last night's game?"

"No I didn't. Your mother was at her club meeting and I was really feeling bad last night. She helped me get in bed before she left and I just didn't feel I could make it into the living room to start the tape."

"Gee dad, why didn't you have Mom program it before she left?"

"You know your mom. She just can't seem to learn how it's done."

"Well for crying out loud," Marc whined. "I wish you two could."

"Just drop it, Marc," his father snapped. "I don't see why you're so hot on seeing yourself on TV anyway. Looks kind of conceited to me!"

How could he explain the importance of the tapes to anyone who did not know of his memory lapses? "O.K. forget it. It's no big deal," he replied pushing his half eaten breakfast away. "We've got practice early today because of the freshman tournament. I may stay after practice and watch the game some. I'll be back later."

"How much later? Are you forgetting that you promised to change the oil in your mother's car?"

"I'll get it done, don't worry."

Marc left the house grumbling to himself. He loved his father and felt sorry for him, but it seemed unfair that the other guys didn't have the kinds of problems he had at home. His main concern right now though was finding a way to fill in the memory gaps from last night's game. He remembered some of it. That was a major breakthrough. Taking the malo hierba in two parts helped quite a bit, but he still couldn't put it all together. He felt sick too, but by now he was getting used to the *morning after* effects of whatever potent drug was bound up in those small, squarish leaves.

Marc glanced at his watch. It was only eight fifteen. Ignoring his headache and nausea, he wheeled the Mustang in a U-turn and headed back the way he had come. "Susan better be up," he said aloud as the small car slipped and slid its way toward her home. An idea was coming fast, and Susan Prell was at the center of it.

Susan answered the doorbell in her robe, but before Marc could say a word she motioned for silence. Marc had forgotten that her dad worked nights and was now sleeping. Susan's mother had already left for work.

Wishing desperately that he hadn't rung the bell, Marc followed Susan on tiptoe into the small kitchen. Susan pointed to a pitcher of juice but Marc shook his head.

"Has that guy come back?" Susan whispered as she gnawed a piece of badly burned toast.

"You mean the guy with the gun? Well not yet anyway." Marc could only barely remember that incident either. "Did he say he was coming back? I can't remember."

"Marc this has gone too far already. I know you've seen doctors but there's something really going wrong in your head! Maybe you'd better try to see a specialist or something."

Marc hesitated, then with a long sigh almost of relief he began. "I think I started to tell you and Biggy last night, but didn't get very far. Is that right?"

"Oh, Marc, everything was happening so fast. I don't know what anybody SAID! I was scared Marc, really scared. That guy could have shot you, or Biggy, or all of us. You have to call the police before he really comes after you. I think Biggy really hurt that guy!"

"Forget him for now. I've got to tell you what's been going on with me lately. I need your promise that nobody, I mean NOBODY hears this. OK?"

"Of course Marc, please tell me, but keep your voice down, alright? I don't want Dad storming in here and throwing you out."

"This is going to be fast Sus, because I've got to be at practice in," Marc checked his watch, "twenty-five minutes."

In exactly twenty-one minutes Susan had heard it all. The malo hierba and how it affected his playing ability, the motorcycle offer by the gambler who called himself Smith, the memory loss and sickness after the game. All of it.

Susan was crying silently as Marc jumped up and sneaked out the door. *"What a mess!"* she thought, *"if only I hadn't promised not to tell I would wake daddy right now!"* Large tears slid down each cheek and fell silently onto the collar of her robe. What could she do? While she felt that this whole business about some sort of magic leaves was obviously ridiculous, Marc's problems were very real.

***

The Christian Athletes Club was meeting again. The starting time was set at 6:30 in order to allow the ball players to finish practice in time to attend.

Janet Compton opened another folded slip of paper from the bowl at her left. She read it aloud. It said: "So Adam and Eve sinned did they? So like why should I have to suffer for that. I had nothing to do with them. It's not fair!"

Coach Jamison had suggested the note-writing method, since many of the kids were reluctant to ask questions in front of the group. It had worked quite well, despite the usual number of jokes and silly stuff that came in also.

"Anybody want to tackle that one?" Janet asked. Nobody did. Chairing the V.C.A.C. was a tough job!

Coach Jamison seated himself on the edge of the desk and looked over the twenty or so faces before him. Then he shocked them all by saying, "You're right, whoever wrote that. It *isn't fair!*"

He cleared his throat and went on. "We can all be thankful that God isn't `fair'. If He were, we would all be lost. No chance for heaven at all."

"Hey Coach," one of Paxton's football players said, "I don't get it. You ain't making no sense."

"Guess I ain't," Jamison grinned, "so let me put it this way. When I was a kid in fifth grade, the teacher made a rule. Any time she was out of the room if we acted up we had to stay in at recess. One time two kids started throwing paper wads. The teacher came back in and saw paper wads on the floor. So we all had to stay in, even though only two kids actually did wrong. Now, would you say that was fair?"

"No way!" someone shouted.

"Think about it," Jamison continued calmly, "the rule was for the class. Since we were all members of the class we all had to pay the penalty."

"I wrote that note Janet read, and I still say it's not fair!" The girl glared at Jamison from the second row.

"O.K. let me finish the story. Our teacher said she liked our class so well that if we just told her we were sorry, SHE would stay in at recess. And she did! That's just like Jesus. Sin has to be punished by someone, so He took the punishment for us."

***

"I know," Sandi pouted, smoothing her cheerleader sweater, "he's big and popular and everything, but where is he going to end up?" It was Monday morning and she and her girlfriends were discussing Bob Marsh, the wrestler. Sandi was getting tired of him. She wished she hadn't had that fight with Marc Cassell, especially now that he was becoming a TV star again.

Coach Jamison had kept after head coach Crites until he finally agreed to show a video tape of the Wellington game. The big screen TV had been set up in the commons area of the cafeteria and nearly the entire student body clapped and cheered at the big moments in the game. When the lunch hour was over not a soul left the big room. As if by previous plan, they simply stayed until the tape ended. Most of the teaching staff, whether free at the time or not, stayed too.

As they left the commons Marc was taking a lot of kidding, but it was meant well. Someone had written $^{\text{Never-Miss-Kid}}$ on his notebook. The nickname was starting to stick.

"Hi Marc, sorry we fought." Sandi was never known to beat around the bush! She took his arm as they climbed the stairs. No one bothered to get a *late admission* slip, since it would have taken several hundred of them to cover all the late students!

"Hi Sandi, how's things?" Marc asked, flattered.

"Great game, Cassell," she purred, not letting go of him. "You were fabulous on TV! Susan says they're going to do another feature on you this week. You'll be FABULOUS!" (Sandi used the world fabulous a lot)

"Sure I will," Marc answered sarcastically. "Coach will probably bench me when we play Addison."

"No he won't. He better not, or I'll be mad at him," Sandi mouthed coyly. She gave Marc's arm a squeeze. "Why don't you ever call me? You still mad?"

"Hey, I'm not mad. I thought you were mad."

Sandi tipped her head prettily, allowing her long hair to fall over one eye.

"Well let's go out some time and neither one of us be mad."

Marc didn't have time to answer, since Sandi popped into her classroom without another word. He glanced all around quickly. "Thank heaven!" he breathed. Susan was nowhere in sight. Neither was the wrestler!

CHAPTER ELEVEN

Mrs. Cassell hurried to the front door, fastening one earring on the way. She snapped on the outside light, and peeked out the side window but didn't recognize the well dressed man standing there. He was wearing a neck brace which held his head immobile. She opened the door a few inches.

"May I help you?"

"Yeah, I think you can. I wanta see Marc Cassell."

Meg hesitated for a moment, then smiled. "I'll bet you're from one of the papers."

"The papers? Oh yeah. Yeah, that's right. I'm from the uh. *uh* ...TRIBUNE. Right, the *Tribune*. I need to see the kid right away."

"I'm sorry, but he isn't here right now."

"I'll wait in the car," the man mumbled. The neck brace squeezed all the way up to his chin, making it difficult for him to speak.

Paul Cassell had wheeled up near the door to see who was there. "The freshman tournament finals are going on tonight," he whispered, peering around his wife at the stranger. "Since he got his car back we never know when he'll be home." Paul tried to laugh a little but the sound died out as in amazement he saw the stranger turn without another word and head for his car.

"Should we have had Marc call him?" Mrs. Cassell asked in bewilderment. "He seemed angry. Do you suppose Marc had told him to come here and then forgot?"

"Who knows," Paul answered wearily. "That kid!" His wheelchair creaked as he began to cough, the sound so weak it could hardly be heard.

"Oh Paul, you shouldn't have come so near to this open door," Meg cried turning his chair. She rubbed his back gently as he trundled slowly into the living room. How she wished to help him along, but she knew he wanted to move himself as much as he could.

Paul Cassell was dying.

***

Biggy watched from the corner of his eye as Marcus licked a tiny, broken piece of leaf from his palm. The big center rolled his eyes in disgust, then bent to re-tie his huge basketball shoes one more time. Coach Crites was pacing nervously, waiting until every player was dressed and ready to listen. As usual Biggy was the last player to look up, signaling that he was ready.

"You guys know about as much about Addison Country Day as I do. They've got more money than we've got. They have better equipment than we have, and they're probably better coached!"

"No!" the team roared in unison.

"Are they better players?"

'No!'

"Are they faster?"

'No!"

"Can we beat them?"

"Yes!" "What?" "Yes!"

"Are we going to beat them?"

"Yes!"

"Then let's do it!"

With a roar the Paxton Pacers thundered out of the locker room, jostling each other to be first up the stairs onto the floor. Marc and Biggy were the very last ones.

Marc had chewed half of a malo hierba leaf in the restroom during half time of the junior varsity game. The tingling was already noticeable in his legs, but he was concerned that the chalky, dry-mouth effect he always noticed before did not seem to be present. As he dribbled and passed around the big circle to start the famous Paxton warm up, he tried to recall exactly how much of the leaf he had chewed up. He could not remember.

"Come on Cassell!" Punchy yelled as Marc bobbled another pass. The Paxton crowd was clapping in unison to the moves their team was making in their pre-game drill. Twice now Marcus had ruined the rhythm, which made the Pacers look foolish. It also brought jeers of delight from Addison Country Day's cheering section.

Marc tried harder and managed to finish the warm-up without further problems. He was worried. Had he taken enough of the drug to continue his fantastic scoring record? Should he try to sneak another piece of leaf right now before the game started?

"Oh man, I've got to quit this crazy stuff," he thought as he flipped a pass to Biggy, "my mind is getting all messed up!"

The warning buzzer sounded. Coach Crites huddled his team, giving them last minute instructions. They slapped hands and trotted onto the court, ready to take on a team their school had been unable to beat for the last six seasons.

Leaning forward on the bench, Crites gnashed at his gum, clapping and yelling as the game started. He had done his best to prepare the Pacers for this particular contest. The coach had personal reasons for wanting to win so badly. No one on the team knew that he had applied for the head basketball coaching job at Addison two years ago, but had been rejected. In addition, there was the humiliation of the yearly beating his teams had taken from the hands of this elite prep school.

"I don't need the big salary they pay anyway," the coach told himself angrily. "All I want now is to beat this bunch of rich, show-offs!" He leaped to his feet screaming as Biggy was called for a personal foul with less than a minute gone in the game. Coach Crites would totally lose his voice before the end of the contest!

Marc was moving well at the point guard position he liked best. Earlier in the week Assistant Coach Jamison had suggested moving the Never-Miss-Kid to forward in order to give him more chances to score. Addison always played a spectacular game on offense, but were not known for a strong defense. The result was almost always a high-scoring contest with Addison Country Day ending up on top. With Marcus Cassell now rivaling Biggy Nelson as the Pacers' top scorer it seemed to Jamison that Cassell should be given every opportunity possible to get into shooting position. Crites said no. He still wanted his guards to be play-makers and safety men against fast break. Scoring, as he saw it, was for the big men underneath. As always he got his way, which kept Marc out front.

Marc was feeling better. The funny taste was now present in his mouth and his legs and finger tips were tingling in the old familiar fashion. He grinned a little, but managed to keep from looking so goofy. "Half a leaf does it!" he exulted, dribbling leisurely as he watched his team jockeying for position. Biggy spun off his defender and called for the ball, but Marc could tell at a glance that Addison's tight zone defense would turn with the pass and bottle the big man up before he could get the shot away. Instead Marc faked right, then floated down the left sidelines drawing the defense toward him. This left Beeler open in the lane. Marc whipped a high pass to the skinny black forward who went up and tapped it in.

The two teams were almost evenly matched. The game started out as a real thriller, the lead changing several times during the first quarter. Addison Country Day presented a balanced scoring attack, usually posting at least three and often five players in double figures. Paxton on the other hand depended heavily on Nelson, Markles, and more recently Cassell to make the baskets. Addison's scouts had picked up on this and were breaking their usual pattern of casual defensive play to key on the Pacers' scoring leaders. Again and again Marc found himself double teamed or forced out of position. In spite of this he was able to break loose or go high over the defense and get his shots away. By halftime he had made two three-pointers, three free throws and two tip-ins for thirteen points. To the delight of the fans he had still not missed, except for a partially blocked shot and one that should have been a goal tending infraction but had not been called by the referee. In spite of his gallant play, Paxton was falling behind.

Crites was talking so fast and loud in the locker room that he was jarring the eardrums of the two Pacers closest to him on the bench. His scouting reports had indicated that Addison's guards were very lax on defense, which was the main reason he had kept Marcus Cassell at guard. What the scouts didn't consider, however, was that in the two games they saw, Addison had not needed to work their guards that hard on defense. They had won both games by over twenty points.

"Cassell," he bellowed, " you and Kelly switch positions for the second half." He stared and Marcus for a second then said, "When you get the ball in there I want you looking for Nelson and Beeler first before you try any of your grandstand plays! Got it?"

"Right, Coach."

"But if you're open and they ain't, shoot the thing!" Crites thundered.

Marc rose from the bench and stood there a minute. Several players turned to stare at him. They knew Crites would have the kid's head if he interrupted his coach.

"Bathroom," Marc told Crites pointing urgently in that direction. Before the coach could answer Marc dashed off to his locker then slipped into one of the stalls. Crites glared after him but with half time almost over he had to continue his instructions.

As the coach rushed his team up the steps, the Never-Miss-Kid bounded past him taking the stairs two at a time. He never stopped running until he was on the other side of the court, as far away from Coach Crites as he could get.

The Pacers had given all they had during the first half but their opponents had surprised them by playing an uncharacteristically tough defensive game, never taking the pressure off Cassell and Nelson. As a result Paxton began the second half trailing by eleven.

Although Cassell preferred the freedom and command of the guard position, Crites had made the proper decision in putting him inside at forward. Punchy Markles was a fine play-maker anyway, so Marc and he were able to do some real magic against a momentarily confused Addison defense.

The other half of the malo hierba leaf was doing its work by the middle of the third quarter. Marc had not taken a shot at the basket during that time, waiting for the drug to give him the edge he desired. Luckily, Biggy was able to get open underneath several times. So

Marc's passes to him appeared to be in response to Coach Crites' instructions.

Once sure of himself however, Cassell began to dominate the game. Taking Punchy's high passes at the top of his leap, Marc would turn in the air and flip the ball over the rim for the score. Or while hanging high if he saw blue jersey's open near the basket he would ram the ball in to them instead. Defensively he was uncanny. While never seeming to hurry, he would be found in the exact spot to take the rebound, whether at the Pacers' basket or that of the big red of Addison.

Country Day's lead was dwindling. By the beginning of the fourth quarter Paxton's fans exploded when a beautiful tip-in by Biggy Nelson tied the score. Cassell added two more goals before Addison could connect again. The red jerseys buckled down and despite their reputation of *poor little rich kids* they were playing really hard, smart basketball. Paxton fans were doing their best to out-shout those of the Country Day rooters, but the Paxton Pacers' unblemished record was not to last.

As an Addison forward drove for the basket for a score that would tie the game up yet again, Punchy went up with him. There was a tangle of arms. The ball dropped through the hoop, but as Punchy and the Addison player dropped to the floor there was an audible "crack" and Punchy lay writhing in pain. Coach Crites and the Paxton team ran out on the floor as the referee signaled for a time out.

The two coaches locked arms with Markles and half carried him off the floor to polite applause from both schools' fans. The trainer helped him down the stairs to the locker room, noticing that the ankle was already swelling alarmingly. There was no doubt that Markles was out for at least the rest of this game. X-rays would need to be taken, as there was the real possibility of a broken ankle.

Tim Wylie, subbing for his injured teammate, played the finest game of his career, but even by moving Cassell back to the guard position, the demoralized Pacers were unable to keep up with a red-hot Addison team.

Paxton lost, eighty-five to seventy-nine.

***

Susan grabbed Marc's arm as he slouched out of the locker room. No one was saying anything. Their perfect record was flawed and there wasn't a thing any one of them could do about it. Only a very few fans and parents had stayed to support the team. Marc shrugged Susan's hands off his arm angrily. "We lost, didn't we? What can I say?"

"You'd have won it if you would have had Punchy the whole game." Susan cried. "But Marc I've got to talk to you."

"Forget it, I'm going home. I'm beat."

"Marcus Cassell, I've got to talk to in private right NOW!" Marc looked at her in surprise. It was unlike her to get so excited.

"O.K., O.K. Let's get in my car."

"No! Not your car! Listen Marc," she lowered her voice and pulled him away from the rest of the team who were straggling silently up the locker room stairs. "You know that guy Biggy beat up last week? Well I saw him at the game tonight. Then when I went for a coke I saw him again! I think he's waiting for you."

"Are you sure it's him!" Marc whispered.

"Of course I'm sure! I'll never forget that creep. And another thing is I think he's got another guy with him. A BIG guy!"

"I'm not afraid of him," Marc stated, but his voice gave him away.

"Where's Biggy?" Susan asked. She looked scared.

"Biggy and some of the other guys went to the hospital already. Coach says Punchy may have a broken ankle. I was planning to go too. What happened to Markles anyway?" Susan was shocked. She peered into Marc's face and demanded, "Don't you remember? He and that big number 42 went down under the basket. You were in the pile-up too. You were right there, Marc!"

"What are we going to do about this character you saw?" Marc asked, changing the subject fast. As usual he could hardly remember anything that had happened earlier in the game. Even the last quarter was fading fast. "Is he outside somewhere do you think?"

"Sure he is! You don't think he came to see the game do you? He'll be hiding out somewhere, him and that big goon he's got with him, and they'll jump you when you come out. You know that Marc. Biggy really crocked him that night. He's not going to just forget that, not to mention the money he probably lost when you didn't go through with that bet."

"O.K. you're right, but what do we do?' Marc whispered desperately, both hands on her shoulders.

The brilliant mercury lights flicked a little. The two kids turned toward the far end of the gym. Nearly everyone was gone by now and the custodians were signaling that they wanted to go home too. Marc and Susan hesitated, then started walking uncertainly toward the darkened lobby.

"I'll handle this," Susan stated emphatically. She started to run toward the janitor, pulling a surprised Marcus Cassell along with her.

"What are you gonna do?"

"You'll see. This has gone too far already." Susan ran up to the janitor and skidded to a stop. "Jimmy I need to make a phone call," she gasped, "is the phone in the lobby working right now?"

"Nah, that thing's been busted since Halloween! You don't happen to know who did it do you?" He peered through thick glasses as each of them in turn.

"Would you please let us into the coach's office then" Susan begged. "I've got to make a call."

"I can't do that and you know it," he grumbled, folding his arms. "Crites told me never to let ANYBODY in there."

"Well what about the ticket office?" Susan mussed the old man's hair a little and gave him her sweetest smile.

"Well maybe, but if anybody hears about it, I'm gone!" He waddled toward the lobby, Marc and Susan staying close behind. The lights flashed on as Marc and Susan quickly scanned the area. No one was in sight. The custodian fished through a huge ring of keys: tried several, and finally unlocked the door. He stood there by the open door watching as Susan picked up the phone. It was clear that he didn't intend to leave.

The phone was dead!

"Is that red truck yours?" Marc asked innocently. He had seen the janitor driving it before.

"Yeah, why?"

"It's pretty neat! What engine you got in that little beauty?" The janitor looked proud. He started toward the main doors.

"Come on out and I'll show you this bomb!"

Marc slapped him on the back. "Hey, it's cold out there man. Why don't you drive it up here by the door? Everybody's probably gone by now."

The janitor looked hard at Marc. "Stay in the lobby, you hear?"

"Sure! Sure! Drive her up here. Let's have a look at that engine."

Susan slammed the ticket booth door and ran to Marc as the janitor left. They kept the lights on and peered fearfully into the darkness.

The red truck came chugging up to the door.

"Come on!" Marc hissed as he yanked Susan out through the exit. He ran up to the passenger side, snatched the door open and jumped in, pulling Susan in too. The driver started to get out to open the hood calling Marc to take a look at the motor he was so proud of. With a clashing of gears Marc finally found reverse and whipped the old pick-up backward. His left knee throbbed in pain as he jammed down on the clutch.

"Hey! Come back here you, you delinquents!" the janitor bawled as his truck jumped erratically forward then swung in a big arc across the empty parking lot. When they were directly beside Marc's Mustang the two kids piled out, leaving the truck door gaping open and the motor throbbing. The Mustang roared into life as Marc pushed the accelerator down hard. Using no lights, they careened out of the parking lot. Lights from a big car flashed across them briefly as Marc wheeled into the nearest alley. Luck was with them. A two-car garage door was open off the narrow street. Without hesitation he whipped the car into the darkened garage and cut the engine.

Susan and Marc sat in dark silence, their hearts beating so fast they hurt. The glow of headlights came creeping down the street. Suddenly a dog began to bark. He was close. A moment later lights came on in the garage. Without a word the kids jumped from the car and ran toward the house, the dog going crazy behind them.

A very angry-looking man met them at the door. Susan talked fast and Marc kept agreeing by nodding his head. The man believed them. Susan called the police. Marc was amazed and impressed that she could give a complete description of the car, and even the license number!

They were safe!

CHAPTER TWELVE

"Keep your voice down!" Meg said, pointing toward her husband's room. They eased out the door into the garage. Marc backed the wagon into the street as his mother stared angrily forward.

"But I'm telling you I had nothing to do with that guy. He came to me and said he'd give me a 450 CC motorcycle if I'd miss a shot on purpose. I didn't do it though." Marc glared sullenly at his mother, almost crossing the center line before jerking his gaze back to the street.

"Well you're grounded anyway. Wrecking your car, being chased by hoodlums! What's next?"

"What about ball practice, Mom? Punchy is out for the rest of the season. If I can't play we won't even make the finals."

Meg half turned toward her son. She was about done in, and now having to make this trip to the police station was the last straw. "Alright, I'll make a little bargain with you on this. You're grounded on everything but basketball. That means no Susan, no youth activities at church or at school, no running to the "T-J CORNER" after practice, nothing but BASKETBALL, understand?"

"But Mom, listen, I'm a senior for crying out loud. I don't want to spend my best year in school grounded half the time!" Marc's voice was rising again.

"Don't shout at me," Meg said. "Your troubles are mostly of your own making. And I'll say one more thing. Your father is a very sick man. He just can't take any more stress. You are not to discuss your grounding with him in any way. AT ALL! and by the way, when are you going to get the oil changed in the wagon?"

The police department seemed in no hurry. Marc found it hard to believe how bored they appeared with the whole business. Almost two hours had gone by.

"You ready?" the sergeant asked. He and Meg remained standing behind Marc who was seated on a low stool directly behind the one-way glass. The paper work done, they were finally ready for the line-up.

"I guess so, Marc answered. He watched the officer press a small button on the wall. A moment later the lights brightened on the other side of the glass. Six men of various sizes and ages trooped sullenly onto the small stage. They stood in a ragged line squinting into the bright lights directed on them.

"You part of this lady?" the cop asked.

"Oh no," Meg whispered, "just my son here."

"They can't hear us in here," he told them grumpily.

"Okay, I see him!" Marc blurted.

"Now kid be SURE before you say anything. A lot depends on a positive identification here. If you ain't absolutely positive, you're not to pick any of them. You got that?"

"Believe me, I see the guy alright! He's the one… "

"Hold it!" Marc jumped at the policeman's command.

"I'm gonna say it one more time. Are you absolutely sure you see the guy who tried to bribe you"?

"Not only that," Marc replied, "the guy also threatened a couple of us with a GUN!" Meg gasped in fright. This was a part of the story she hadn't heard. "Alright, which one is he?"

"Third from the left end. The one with the neck brace."

The cop's whole attitude instantly changed. Grinning broadly he clapped Marc on the back. "Good job kid, good job! That guy won't be bothering you or anybody else for quite a while! Go home and forget him."

As soon as they were home, Marc hurried into the den, slammed his lanky frame into an easy chair, and picked up the remote. He had programmed the V.C.R. himself. The tape of last night's game was ready to go.

He ran the entire Madison contest through three times, not even stopping for the early supper his mother brought him on a tray. She did not speak, just set it down and left. Meg didn't ask him to help her get Paul into the station wagon, but he did.

She was crying. This time Marc's father was going back to the hospital to stay a while. It was unclear what would happen next. Both Marc and Meg assured each other that Paul would be able to come home before too long. Keeping their spirits up for Paul's benefit was becoming harder and harder.

Marc clicked off the set with a groan that sounded very loud in the empty house. Three times seeing the final losing score was three times too many! But at least he now could discuss what had happened at the game.

***

He climbed out of the car and carried the dishes to the kitchen. On the way back to the den he picked up his book bag and took out his "Amateur Archaeologist's Hand-book." Flipping through the pages allowed the MALO HIERBA to flutter out. Some of them fell to pieces, but Marc carefully gathered up every fragment. He placed each whole leaf in an individual envelope and slipped them back between the pages. Next he stretched a heavy rubber band around the small volume.

There were six leaves left. A tear fell on the cover as the boy stared at the fat book on the floor between his feet. Until that moment he had not realized he was crying. His head ached, he was mildly nauseous, and only blurred images remained from most of the games he had played.

He needed to talk to someone very badly. The house was too quiet. He missed the big Labrador they used to have. Charger was always there when you were down, or even if you were up, for that matter! They had put Charger out on their uncle's farm six months ago because the doctors suspected that Marc's father was allergic to something in the dog's coat.

Marc got up and headed for the phone. He was grounded but Susan wasn't! It didn't take her long to get there.

For awhile they talked about the game, Punchy's injuries, and school. Finally though, Marc started in on his troubles. He opened the archaeology book and carefully took out one of the envelopes.

"See this leaf? It's what makes me able to hit so well in the ball games. I was going to tell Biggy and everyone the night we fought with that gambler, but, you know … we got kind of busy there for a while!

"Oh yeah! Sure! You just look at that little brown leaf and you become the 'Never-Miss-Kid', right? Do you say the magic word too? Where's your red suit with the big red S on it? Besides," she continued, "you told me all about this before! Don't you remember? I didn't believe it then, and I don't believe it NOW!"

Marc looked at her hard. His brows drew down and bright spots of pink blossomed on each cheek. Susan knew the signs. She punched him on the arm lightly. "Come on Marc," she chided, "you don't expect me to swallow this stuff do you? You just think these things help you and so you play better. Right?"

Marc started in. The more he told her, the faster the words came pouring out. Susan was astounded. For the first time she was forced to accept the truth of it all. She could only say, "Marc, oh Marc!" over and over at every juncture in his confession. She held one of the MALO HIERBA leaves in one hand and simply stared at the innocent looking little piece of vegetation. *The whole story was incredible!*

She did her best to comfort her boyfriend, but finally had to tell Marc she was expected at home. She always helped her mother on Saturday afternoons. "I'll be grounded too if I don't get back pretty quick," she moaned. Still holding the leaf, she gave Marc a quick hug and ran for the front door.

The MALO HIERBA leaf, forgotten, lay jammed in the bottom of her jacket pocket.

***

Assistant Coach Jamison was smiling broadly. He leaned forward across the battered desk in his tiny office. Marc stood before him, hands in his pockets as the big man with the aviator sunglasses sauntered into the room.

"Marc, meet James Lee Dunn," Jamison said, rising from the old swivel chair. "Mr. Dunn, this is our 'Never-Miss-Kid' right here."

They shook hands, Marc feeling a little embarrassed but pleased to meet the former State star in person. The interview had been set up two days before, and was being conducted just before varsity practice early on Wednesday afternoon.

"Well kid, you're in all the papers," the big man rumbled. "I know you've got to get dressed for practice pretty soon so I won't mess you around." Marc nodded, saying nothing.

"You know State's basketball coach?" Dunn asked, looking the boy over.

"Lyberger?" Marc laughed, "I guess I wouldn't be much of a sports fan if I didn't know who HE is!"

"Yeah, I guess not. Well he sends me around to take a look at some of the prep school stand-outs we hear about. I'll be doing double duty here at Paxton. I want to catch a game or two if I can."

"Double duty?" Coach Jamison asked.

"Right Coach. State has been interested in Paxton's big guy, Nelson, since last season, but lately we've been hearing some pretty unbelievable things about your man Cassell."

So you'll be watching both Nelson and Cassell?" Jamison acted surprised, but he wasn't really. Biggy had had some small college scouts looking him over since the middle of last year, but this was different. He couldn't think of anyone in this league who wouldn't jump at the chance to get a scholarship at a state university.

Marc spoke for the first time. "Suppose you take us, or one of us at least, what's involved? I mean college costs, tuition, dorm fees, you know."

Coach Crites appeared at the door in time to hear Marc's question. He stood leaning against the door frame, listening. There was hardly room for another person in the converted janitor's closet that had been given to Jamison for his *office*.

The scout nodded to coach Crites, then turned back to Marc. "Anyone who signs a letter of intent with us gets a full ride for a year. Ninety-nine percent of the time the kid will play on the freshman squad only. You make or break that year."

"So you're back, Dunn," Crites said, his lips twisted in a wry smile, "are you going to sign this boy right here and now?"

"Not RIGHT now, but maybe after I see a game or two live. I've reviewed the two tapes you sent me, but I like to get my info first hand."

Marc shot a surprised look at Crites. So he was the one who had given State their first glimpse! Maybe Coach didn't hate him after all.

"Well good luck, but don't get these kids' hopes up too high," Crites said as he sauntered away, "we've still got two more games, then the tournament!"

Dunn put a hand on Marc's shoulder. "You guys keep playing like you've been and there's a good chance I'll get to watch you at State's coliseum. That's where the finals are played you know." He handed Marc a packet of promotional material.

"I know," Marc replied dryly. Was there anyone in this state who DIDN'T know where the final two championship games were held?

"We'll have to play a lot better than our last one," Jamison said, rising to leave.

"I read about that game. It even made the CAPITOL REVIEW. Mr. Cassell here is getting your Pacers some real publicity! Too bad about your guard. What's his name again?"

"Markles," Marc replied, "he may be out for the rest of the season."

"Yeah I heard," Dunn said squeezing out of the small door. "I kind of wanted to consider him too, but Lyberger says, 'too small'. And now that he's on the injured list I guess that clinches it."

Marc walked along beside the big State scout. Jamison hurried off to the locker room.

"You shouldn't give up on Punchy yet," Marc said earnestly, "he's really great. He'll have that ankle in shape in a couple of months and be ready to go next season."

"Who's 'Punchy'?"

"Markles, Punchy Markles."

"Maybe kid, maybe. We'll see." He started up the stairs then turned to yell at Marc. "Think your coach would mind if I watch some of tonight's practice?" Mark looked around. "I don't know. You better ask HIM before you do."

Laughing, the scout headed on into the gym. "Same old Crites, huh?" he said, opening the door.

Marc pursed his lips angrily. He didn't want to be scouted in PRACTICE! Without the help of his MALO HIERBA, he would only look like what he was; a skinny, small town kid two inches over six feet who loved the game of basketball. *"Well that's show biz!"* he told himself, entering the locker room. The one good thing was that the scout was almost sure to come back for their final home game, since he wanted to see Biggy as well.

"Shoot it, 'Never-Miss'!" Crites screamed as once again Marc passed off rather than take the shot. Some of the guys laughed. They knew the scout was there, and they also knew why Marc wasn't shooting. Marc raised a hand to signal that he'd heard his coach. He shot a glance at the stands where the State University man sat sprawled across two seats. He had a small notepad on one thick knee, but so far Marc hadn't seen him make a mark on it.

The practice went on. Marc was still being careful not to shoot anything that he wasn't reasonably sure would go in. Luckily for him, Crites was working on defense most of the evening. This made it easy for Cassell to maintain the appearance of never missing, even in practice.

Crites was pulling Beeler physically around the court, railing on him to move in the way he had been coached. Marc stole another glance up into the darkened seats, but the scout was gone.

***

Jefferson was a pushover. Though it was a league game, even Crites knew the Pacers had it won shortly after half-time. He pulled several varsity players, saving them for the Saturday night contest to follow. Biggy stayed in the game and had the best offensive night of his career, scoring forty-four points against the smaller and almost totally demoralized Jefferson cagers.

Marc was hardly able to sit on the bench! He had scored sixteen points before Crites took him out. Three of his goals were spectacular three-pointers, as once again one-half of a MALO HIERBA did its work. He was still to miss a single shot at the basket in regular game play.

Bouncing up and down as he whistled through his teeth, Marc craned his neck and eyed the small crowd of Jefferson fans. Then he saw him. Mr. Bunn was slouched comfortably in the half empty visitors' section, one leg hanging over the seat-back before him. His pad was once again balanced on the other knee.

Marc kept sneaking looks at the scout, even though he had to turn away from the game to do it. He felt great! The remaining portion of the leaf he had secretly chewed during half-time was kicking in hard. The trouble was he was not on the floor, and it appeared that none of the varsity would be put back in the game. How he wanted to PLAY!

"Hey Coach," Marc suddenly yelled, his feet dancing a fast rhythm on the floor, "put me in, will you? I want to play!" The boy laughed and slapped a bobbing thigh as he waited for Crites to answer.

"Relax!" the coach snarled, tearing his eyes away from the game for a minute.

"You'll go in if I say so! Watch the game."

Coach Jamison, sitting on Crites' right, nudged the head coach with an elbow. He jerked his head in Cassell's direction and rolled his eyes. Crites nodded then gave his attention back to the game in progress. Jamison had not needed to call his attention to the Never-Miss-Kid. Crites had been noticing the signs too. Anybody who really observed the tall guard, especially when he was not in the game, could hardly miss the erratic, compulsive behavior the kid displayed.

"Something," Crites told himself *"has to be done, but I'm going to wait to do it until after the tournament. I can use any kid who can hit the way he does, WHATEVER he's on! I'll deal with our Never-Miss- Kid after the season!"*

The game dragged on with Jefferson falling further and further behind. Biggy was loose underneath nearly half the time. Even the third string Pacers could easily give him the kind of lead passes and high lofters that made him look like a pro. Of all the nights for a scout to be watching, Biggy figured it couldn't be better than this.

Biggy did not know James Lee Bunn! He had been a fine player for state many years back, then enjoyed a few years in the pros. Now scouting, he was not fooled by watching a talented prep schooler looking like a million dollars when playing against a bunch of losers. He would have to come back to watch the big center when he had some competition.

Becoming increasingly bored with the non-contest he had to endure, Bunn found his attention drawn more and more to number forty-four, who was bouncing around on the bench. He was puzzled. The kid had certainly showed him some spectacular shooting while he was in the game. The Paxton fans obviously loved him and Bunn could see why. Still, Cassell had appeared so hyper-active that the scout had to wonder how he, like the big center Nelson, would react in a really tight, intensive ball game.

"Tomorrow night too, I guess," Bunn told himself. He had hoped to get back to the city and have a night at home for a change, but he certainly couldn't hand Lyberger a scouting report on either of the two Paxton players based on this ridiculous contest! With most of the fourth quarter still to play he gathered up his things and ambled toward the exit. Some fans from both teams were doing the same.

"You're James Lee Bunn aren't you?" an older Paxton fan smiled up at him. "In the flesh. A lot of flesh!" Bunn laughed. "Some game huh?"

"Not much of a contest," the man agreed, grinning amiably.

"Well," the old man said as they left the steamy gym, "tomorrow night won't be no turkey shoot like this one! Paxton will be lucky to pull it off. You scouting some-body?"

"Aw you know, just looking them over," Bunn hedged. He knew better than to start any rumors. Enough of them were going around already!

A half hour later Bunn sat quietly in a nearly deserted Paxton, Indiana coffee shop. Nelson, the kid they called "Biggy," he was certain would get his chance at State.

The player he was becoming more and more interested in however was Marcus Cassell. This Never-Miss-Kid might be just what the dwindling crowds at State could use next season. He sipped at his second cup of coffee and let his mind wander. *"Sup-pose, just suppose,"* he mused, *"Lyberger would let that kid play on the varsity. Just a game or two! If he keeps up this one hundred percent shooting, and Paxton makes it to the state finals, EVERYBODY would have to see this guy!"* He threw a bill on the counter and deep in thought, headed for the door. He had a proposal to make which he felt pretty sure coach Lyberger and the rest of the State coaching staff would find very interesting, but he still needed to see tomorrow night's game.

CHAPTER THIRTEEN

"Marcus, it's for you!" Meg called up the stairs. She hoped the phone call would get him down at last. Here it was almost eleven and he'd not even had his breakfast yet!

"Susan?" he asked, stumbling down the steps.

"I don't think so. It didn't sound like Susan, but she didn't give her name." Meg stared at her son. It seemed he could hardly walk to the phone! His face was flushed and she could see his left eyelid fluttering erratically. "Are you sick again?" she whispered, handing him the phone.

Marc didn't answer. He fell into a kitchen chair.

"Hello," he croaked.

"Hi Kid, guess who?"

Marcus pulled the receiver away from his ear as the upbeat but very loud cheerleader's voice came blasting through.

"Hi Sandi, what's happening?" Marc answered, accepting a glass of juice from his mother. It seemed to him that his mom lingered near the phone a lot longer than was really necessary. He gave her a look but still she brought him a piece of cold toast before reluctantly leaving the kitchen.

"I hear you're getting a basketball scholarship to State next year," Sandi gushed.

"Sure! I'm going to start every game and help coach too," Marc replied. Sandi giggled.

"Word gets around fast," Marc said, almost gagging on the cold toast. He gave up after a bite or two. He really didn't feel like talking but for Sandi he was making a real effort. Of course with her, conversing was hardly a problem. She never seemed to run down!

"I liked your picture in the Clarion," Sandi babbled on, "you looked so TALL and your hair, I just love the way you flip that up in front. Do you spray it before every game?" Before Marc could answer she was gone again. "Alisha said you're going to be in some big magazine. Are you? Really?"

"Well mom got a phone call the other day from NOW SPORTS, INC., but they didn't say for sure..."

"Oh Marc that's NEAT!" Sandi breathed. "When they come do you suppose I could watch or something? You know I've always wanted to be a writer for some magazine. I mean some big one like... like... which one was it you said was coming?"

"I guess it would be O.K. Sandi, but they didn't really set a date. Coach Crites will really be mad too I suppose. He's trying to keep everything real cool until tournament time."

"Thanks Marc, you're so NEAT! How many shots is it now without a miss?" "Eighty-eight is what they tell me, but I don't know how long it will keep on."

"Oh come on! You'll keep on making them. And Marc, really try not to miss until that magazine guy comes. And don't forget to tell me as soon as you know when they'll be here, because I really DO want to watch the pictures and that stuff."

"Well sure I'll let you know, but Crites may not ..."

"Forget Crites! He can't tell you who can be at your picture day thing or whatever it is. Call me, OK?" She chatted on, flirting shamelessly.

Marc was feeling better. The nausea was clearing up and the rubbery feeling in his legs seemed to be fading. He was glad there was no practice, since there was a game coming up that night.

When Sandi finally wound down she suggested they see a movie together. He told her he was still grounded. When the cheerleader then suggested a night the following week he had to tell her that Coach Crites had absolutely forbidden any social activities during the week before tournament. She pouted a little but finally hung up. Marc hurried into the den, but a frantic search produced no game video. His mother had either forgotten or hadn't bothered to set it up.

He went into the kitchen to find something to eat. Munching away, he opened his ARCHAEOLOGY HANDBOOK and flipped out one of the few remaining envelopes. He laid it beside his sandwich, but after a few minutes he shoved it under the book. Just looking at the thing was making him sick again!

***

"Go ahead, pull out a question," CAC president Janet challenged. Biggy thrust a huge paw into the coffee can. He waved the slip of paper above his head then let it flutter to the floor. "Why don't you read it?" Janet asked the big ball player.
"O.K. It says, 'Is the earth and everything REALLY that old or not?'
"Thanks Biggy. If no one else wants to tackle that one I'll try it, OK?"
Coach Jamison smiled his agreement. He was a little surprised, but glad to see the club president beginning to take more leadership.
What no one in the CAC organization knew was that Janet had written all of the notes in the can herself! Every one had the same topic. She had done her homework, and she was READY!
"We've all seen those fantastic figures about how old the world is. Well I believe it's not nearly that old. I believe that God made everything in six regular days just like the Bible says in Genesis. I know the mountains, rocks, and stuff sure look old, but that's just how God made them."
"Hey Janet, you don't mean ... "
"Come on Shari, let me finish. Then I'll take any questions. Like when God made Adam. I'd guess maybe Adam would look like he was about 18 or 20 years old. He would have to have had mature muscles, bones and everything just like an adult, one second after God brought him alive.
God had already made the animals, birds, fish, and all. Those things would need lakes to swim in, trees to nest in, grass to eat, and well, whatever. So everything probably looked real old, but was actually brand new. Any questions?"
"I've got a question."

"Shoot!"

"In earth science class last year we had to study about coral. You know the stuff that used to be like. well ... little shells all stuck together."

"Sure, I studied that my freshman year too," Janet responded. "So what's your question?"

"Those things got so big they even made ISLANDS. That HAD to take millions of years didn't it?"

"Not necessarily Curt. When God created the sea creatures a lot of them live in and around those coral reefs. They had to have those things ready right away so they would have a place to go."

"So God made that stuff all at once, just like it had been there about a zillion years?" Curt asked.

Janet paused a minute then said, "Yes, that's what I believe."

There were no further questions.

Janet grabbed the coffee can and took it with her to make sure that no one looked into it!

CHAPTER FOURTEEN

The team gave a ragged cheer as Punchy hobbled into the locker room. He was using only one crutch, but it was obvious that he was unable to put much weight on the leg.

Markles, embarrassed, yelled, "Shut up you weirdos!" They all laughed and continued suiting up for the game.

Crites came striding into the room like the commander that he was. The loud talk and horseplay tapered off fast. In a moment it was totally silent in the room. Those still tying their shoes or adding a little resin to their fingers did it noiselessly. Still the man did not speak. The players sneaked glances at him as he moved slowly back until he was leaning against the door to his office. When he caught their eye they would quickly look away. *Crites on the rampage was something they were used to, but Crites in silence was somehow even more devastating!*

Finally he began. "Last night is history. Forget last night. Last night is OVER!" Having started out in a voice quite soft, his last word was almost a scream. Several Pacers jumped at the sound. Some of the seniors felt that the coach had made his point!

"Now it's tonight." his voice had again dropped to something only slightly above a whisper. "This game will determine whether we get top seed in the tournament. We have to have this game." His eyes cut around the silent room slowly, not resting until he had made eye contact with every player there. "I'm asking for your best," he said.

Marc could never remember his coach asking them for anything in the four years he had been on the Pacer squad. No one else could either, and they were all duly impressed. Each ball player felt the coach had spoken to him personally, and that the man was serious. Not one boy felt that Crites was just being theatrical. Each one vowed calmly and silently that he would do his best.

Crites knew how to coach high school kids.

Eyes straight ahead and shining, they filed out of the locker room without a word. They were shocked at the roar which greeted them as they took the floor. The noise seemed almost a sacrilege when associated with something as important as this contest.

Half a MALO HIERBA leaf was just about right, but Marc could tell their effect on him was not as strong as it had been when the season started. All the symptoms were there, but now he was able to control himself a lot better. What really bothered him was his memory. This particular effect of the drug was, if anything, getting worse with every leaf. Marcus Cassell, however, was a high school senior. In two months he would reach his eighteenth birthday. He had a good chance for a full scholarship at a state university. Articles and pictures of him were appearing more and more regularly in the papers. What was a little temporary, he hoped, memory loss compared to all of that?

The warm-up over, Crites and Jamison huddled with the entire team. The head coach amazed them once again. Rather than his usual saliva-spraying-frenzied-last-minute screaming session, he moved from player to player. He said not a single word to any one of them. Instead he extended his right hand and formally shook hands with each one in turn.

When Crites faced Biggy Nelson he started to shake with him, then suddenly threw both arms around the huge center and gave him a bear hug. Biggy had no idea what to do with all this!

Coach sat down. The second stringers sat too as the starters headed for the center circle. Each one had his own thoughts, but there was no question about the desire to win. Never had they felt so close to each other. At this moment they were more attached to each other than to their own families.

"What a great coach!" Marc thought as he jostled the forward for a favorable spot at the tip-off He could only wonder how a man you could gladly murder on one day could make you want to give him a hug on another!

Biggy got the tip and the final game of the regular season was underway. Marc, once again at the point, was handling the ball. Both the Pacers and the Bearcats of Cameron Academy were playing ultra-conservative ball. Each respected the other, and neither team was about to do something stupid. With nearly identical records, (Cameron had only lost two games)not only was the league championship at stake but also the all-important bye in the top bracket of the regional tournament. Although Paxton, with only a single loss, was assured of at least a tie for the league trophy, Crites had made it abundantly clear that he had no intention of sharing that honor with anyone!

The TV cameras were rolling as Marcus Cassell, the "Never-Miss-Kid," made his first weaving drive to the basket. Few people in the packed Academy gym had seen the unique move that the Paxton guard was using to penetrate the Bearcat defense. One astute sports writer, known for his coined words and phrases, would dub Marc's drives "the double split." It was a pretty accurate description too, since it almost appeared that the willowy guard's body would be heading in one direction while one long, sinewy arm and the dribbled basketball went another. By the time his confused defenders finally saw where he was actually going, Marc was usually sprinting into the bunny shot zone!

Unlike most high school players Marc was able to analyze the game as it developed and at the same time remain virtually unaware of his surroundings. The crowd noises, shouts from the bench, even the antics of the cheerleaders hardly registered with him. The MALO HIERBA was without doubt the reason he could do this.

Despite his unorthodox dribbling and lightning drives Marc was stopped on his first two attempts. The Cameron defense was well coached. In addition, they had spent many hours watching the films of Paxton's previous games. With the explosive Punchy Markles on the injured list they felt even freer to concentrate on Cassell and Nelson. During the first three minutes they were able to hold both Pacer standouts scoreless. Luckily, Beeler was hot on this crucial night. His two shots close in had kept the Pacers even with Cameron, who had also scored twice.

Crites called for a time out. His beady, black eyes seemed ready to pop from his skull as he pounced on Biggy and the two forwards.

"You've go to MOVE in there," he gasped, "the guards can't do it all! Biggy, get out of the coffin corner. Move man, MOVE!"

The kindly, soft spoken, hand shaking Crites had disappeared. In his place was a fire breathing dragon going a little crazy!

"For once," Marc thought, "he's not on MY case!"

"Cassell!" Crites snapped, whirling on his grinning guard, "enough of the slow down, cautious stuff! Turn it on, man. Turn it ON!"

"Guess I spoke too soon," Marc thought as he loped back onto the court. "If he wants speed, he's GOT it!"

Marc repeated his coach's admonition over and over as play resumed. He had learned earlier in the season that by doing so, and with only half a MALO HIERBA leaf he could keep Crites' instructions in mind for quite a few minutes

Cameron scored again. Raymond Klear passed off to Marc and he was off and running. His dribbling was a sight for wonder. Running full speed one moment, he would slack off, leaving his opponent off balance and out of position. Instantly then he was at top speed again, cutting in and out of the pack, but untouched by anyone.

Eight feet out he went up for the shot. The ball rimmed the basket but did not drop. Horrified, Marc stared at the ball as it caromed off the backboard. He did not go for the rebound, he didn't pursue when the Bearcats took it down to their basket. In daze he found himself standing on Paxton's end of the court all alone.

"I missed," he said aloud.

Fans from both schools were erupting. Paxton with groans and growls, Cameron with what could only be called a sustained scream of joy. The Never-Miss-Kid had at last proved his humanity!

Cameras were clicking and the video units were rolling. Every eye and every piece of equipment was on the senior guard from Paxton High.

Two reporters left the gym on the run, each hoping to be first with the classic picture of the most famous prep school player in the country stunned by his first miss in eighty-eight shots at the basket.

Coming out of his daze at last, Marc raced to the far end in an attempt to take up his assigned defensive position. He was too late.

Cameron had not only scored, but taking advantage of what amounted to a four man defense had stolen Paxton's in-bounds pass as well. Marc came flashing into the play. An angry scowl had replaced his usual silly grin.

Driving hard, Marcus penetrated the Cameron offense. Keying on their point man he feinted toward him while watching the reaction. When the guard flinched Marc saw his opponent's right arm go back. Cassell went high and intercepted the intended pass before it had traveled two feet through the air. Gritting his teeth he hurled himself toward the far end. His dribbling was a blur as he took it in all alone.

During the next three minutes he scored two three pointers and made a key rebound, which caused Cameron to call time out.

"Glad you missed!" Crites screamed above the crowd. He was sweating as much as any player on the team. His tie hung halfway down his shirt front and his spiky hair was a bird's nest of disarray. "Now you can forget your stupid RECORD!" he yelled pulling Marc up into his face. "Play ball man! Play BALL! We need this win. Gotta have it man!" The coach swung away from Marc and started in on the other four. But as the team gripped hands before taking the court again, he pulled Marc back. "Go hard buddy!" he said in an almost normal voice. "Play your kind of ball! Do whatever it takes, but help us win this one, you hear?" Marc gulped and nodded, He wished it were half time.

The MALO HIERBA was wearing off fast. He needed that other half of a leaf Marc was playing well, but the edge he always counted on was fading. He knew what he had to do, and it had to be done fast.

Cassell bulled his way under the bucket, leaving his assigned man free. Cameron passed in to their lanky center. The big man fumbled the pass and both Biggy and Marcus went after it. There was tangle which eventually included half the players on the court. Whistles blasting, the refs pulled bodies apart and grabbed the ball. One Paxton player did not get up.

Marc lay rocking on the hardwood, his left knee drawn up to his chest. Biggy hooked a black hand under one armpit to lift his teammate to his feet. Very few people saw what Biggy saw next. Marc clamped a hand over his face as if in pain, but his right eye was exposed enough to give Biggy a big, very obvious WINK. Gently, Biggy lowered the smaller man back to the floor.

Both Crites and Coach Jamison were kneeling by their boy. Official time-out was called. Paxton fans were horrified, but the Cameron stands were going crazy. Not only had the much touted Never-Miss-Kid finally missed, but it looked as if he was now out of this crucial game.

"Get me to the locker room!" Marc gasped, pretending to be nearly unable to rise. "All I need is this knee taped up and I can get right back in."

"I'll take him down," Coach Jamison yelled. He was one of the few who had seen the look which passed between Biggy and Marcus. Jamison had a good idea what was going on, and he meant to be in on it. To him there was a more important issue here than even the outcome of this ball game.

It was to Cameron's credit that many of their fans joined those of Paxton to give the young player a standing ovation as he was half carried off the floor.

In the locker room, Marc knew he had to get the assistant coach distracted. "Coach," he gasped, "you've got to go up and get my warm-up jersey. There's a pill in one of the pockets that I've got to take right now."

"This is IT!" Jamison thought as he bounded up the stairs. "Now we'll see what this kid is into!"

The moment the door closed Marc leaped to his feet and ripped open his locker. He dug one sweating hand into the left jacket pocket and grabbed the gum wrapper. Ripping it open he shook out the crumbling pieces of leaf. He crammed them into his mouth and began to chew madly.

"There's nothing in your pockets," Jamison yelled, shoving Marc's jersey in his face, "I checked them both."

"Oh I must have forgot," Marc said in consternation. "Tell you what coach. Give me an ace bandage and I'll wrap this knee myself.

Go up and tell Crites I want back in the game!" Jamison looked long and hard at Cassell, then shrugging his shoulders raced back to the gym.

Marc breathed a great sigh of relief. In another few minutes he would be ready to tear into them again!

Crites had other ideas. Unaware of the fake Marc was pulling, he made him sit out the remainder of the second quarter, saving him, as he thought, for the second half. Paxton was down by fourteen.

Marc sat at the bench and tried to look hurt, but not TOO hurt! Nothing could have worked better for him. Just before the third period started he did a few knee-bends for his coach to show he was *almost* as good as new. Crites sent him into the game. Cameron fans booed and stamped, protesting the obvious *grandstanding* by Paxton's number forty-four. Coach Jamison noted that there was also some booing from the Pacer fans!

Paxton won it by four.

***

"Oh-Oh!" Marc thought as he headed toward his locker. It was Monday morning and until this moment he had been feeling good. The, by now expected post-game, nausea was all cleared up. His name and picture were in all the papers, and the local TV station had done another feature on him. Unfortunately, the latest coverage had concentrated on his first missed shot in the Cameron game.

All these good thoughts went flying as he saw the two girls nose-to-nose by Susan's locker. He could hear them going at each other before he was even close.

"You did NOT!" Susan cried, her eyes blazing. "You never asked me how I felt or what Marc and I had going."

"I don't care what you what say, it's what really happens that counts!" Sandi Myles' statement made no real sense, but both girls kept right on at each other. Several girls were hanging around the two by now, secretly happy to have something going to relieve the boredom of a Monday morning at school.

Marc tried to slip away, but Sandi spotted him and yelled his name. Warily he sidled up to them, well aware that the little crowd was growing, drawn in by the girls' increasingly loud voices. Grabbing his elbow, Sandi pulled Marc into the center of the circle. "Let's hear it from you right now!" she demanded. "Who's it going to be, `Susan the wimp' or me?"

"Cut it out Sandi," Marc replied, his voice hardly above a whisper. "Anyway I thought you were back with Marsh."

Susan started to cry. "I hate you Marcus Cassell! Go on. Start up with her! I hope you do. You've got the big head anyway. Just don't call me anymore and don't come crying when you run out of your special little stuff that makes you the 'Never-Miss Kid'!"

She said Marc's nickname with a snear. She turned to her unopened locker. Several of her girlfriends moved closer to her, giving Marc hate stares as they did so.

"Let's go," Sandi said triumphantly. Already she had assumed victory in the fight. She was not at all worried. *Susan Prell was no real competition anyway. Everyone would be talking about the fight too. She loved attention. She craved it. What was life worth if nobody ever NOTICED you?"*

***

The CAC had cancelled two meetings. Once because school was closed for bad weather, and more recently due to excitement over the Paxton boys' basketball successes.

Katie from the girls' basketball team offered to take a turn at drawing a question from the coffee can. Her team had not fared very well during their season, which preceded that of the boys. With a record of four and fourteen, they were considering it a "rebuilding year"!

"I can hardly read this scribbling," she growled, peering at the wrinkled piece of notebook paper she had drawn. "I think it says, `what about them dinosaurs?' Dinosaurs isn't spelled right either."

Laughing, the kids peered this way and that, looking for the red face that would give the culprit away. Whoever had written the note

THE KID WHO COULDN'T MISS

was a good actor or actress however, as no one seemed to be indicated.

"Well who wants to answer this?" Janet queried crossly. She didn't feel capable, and was hoping one of the club members would offer some ideas or opinions. When no one spoke up, she glanced hopefully at Coach Jamison, who was grading some papers in a back row seat.

"Anyone?" he asked, coming forward. Still no one raised a hand.

"Dinosaurs eh? Well how long ago they existed puzzled me for a long while too. But then I read about a discovery along the Paluxy River, near Glen Rose, Texas. As I'm sure most of you know, the footprints of dinosaurs are sometimes found in stone. Evolutionists understandably viewed this as evidence that these creatures roamed the earth before the mud they stepped in hardened into stone. They therefore concluded that dinosaurs lived millions of years before humans came on the scene.

All of this changed for me when I read about these archaeologists who discovered HUMAN footprints in the stone right along with those of dinosaurs!"

"I don't believe that."

Jamison was surprised by the challenge from a boy lounging in the second row.

He smiled a little. "I don't blame you," he said, "I wouldn't have believed it either except for the evidence given. There were plenty of dinosaur tracks in the lime-stone ledges along the river. Then somebody recognized human footprints too. Eminent archaeologists were contacted. One was an Australian who was a member of one of the most prestigious archaeological organizations in the world. They did a very thorough examination of the evidence."

"Maybe you could bring those books to one of our coming meetings," Janet said.

"Sure I will. When you read these books and see the photos in them I'm sure you'll be just as convinced as I am. The human prints are there, right beside the dinosaurs. There were even a few that were down IN the dinosaur tracks! To me that proves that men and dinosaurs existed at the same time. Of course it's easy for me to think that way since I believe the Bible account that God created everything within six regular days.

"I want to see those books," the original challenger stated.

"I'll have them on my desk tomorrow for you or anyone to read. Incidentally, they had local TV coverage during the dig. They made a movie of it too. The books are titled, FOOTPRINTS AND THE STONES OF TIME, and DINOSAUR. Both are by Carl E. Baugh, Ph. D, and Dr. Clifford Wilson."

"Our time's about up," Janet reminded him.

"Just let me say one more thing Janet. These discussions and questions have been great. I've enjoyed them a lot. But remember that we don't all have to agree on everything. Only one thing really counts. Whatever else you believe, or don't believe, what's necessary is belief in Christ, His death and resurrection, and the fact that His shed blood paid for our sins. If we accept Him as our savior we'll go to heaven when we die. Any questions?"

There were no questions.

***

"So you missed a couple times in games lately. Big deal!" Sandi was aglow as she clung to Marc's arm on the way to class. "I heard you got scouted by State again, right?"

"Biggy too," Marc mumbled. "I wish Markles was healthy. We might all three get to go next year!"

"Forget THEM!" Sandi snapped. "When's the interview with 'Now Sports'?"

"I told you it's after practice Tuesday," Marc replied, irritation plainly evident in his voice.

"Can I come?"

"Sure. It's open. Anybody can be there. It'll be in the old gym at about 5:30."

"Great! I'll wear my new cheerleading outfit. The boosters bought us all new ones to wear for the championship games."

"I saw," Marc grunted. His eyes roved the crowed hall, looking for Susan. She was not to be seen.

***

Marc was a little surprised that his interviewer was a bright eyed young lady who didn't look much older than Susan or Sandi. They were seated at a small table which was used for ticket sales at Junior Varsity games and other such minor events held at Paxton's *old gym*. Dressed in a very conservative skirt and blouse, the girl looked completely relaxed and interested.

"What is your opinion about your head coach? Does he really know what he's doing?"

Marc was stunned. He was also a little angry. *What kind of a question was THAT?* "He's a good coach," he answered, glancing around at the small but growing group of students and fans who had learned of the interview and had come to watch.

"By 'good' would you say he is great or just OK? Tell me how you really feel."

Marc noticed Sandi Myles moving closer and closer to the table. When she was standing almost at his elbow he half turned to her, glad for a chance to gather his wits.

"This here is Sandi. She's captain of our cheerleading squad." Sandi's smile was dazzling as she played up instantly to the feature writer.

Miss Crisinsky appraised the cheerleader coolly. She did not smile. "Are you and Marc going together?" she asked mildly, not taking the hand Sandi had thrust at her.

"Oh YEAH!" Sandi purred, letting one hand rest familiarly on Marc's shoulder. "We've been together forEVER! Don't you think he's just FABulous?"

"Well I don't know. I've hardly got two words out of him so far," she replied turning her gaze back on the boy. "We were talking about your coach, right Marc?"

"He's a great coach. We'd never have made the finals without a coach like Crites."

"Did you know that Marc hardly ever misses the basket?" Sandi shrilled. "You should see him play, he's..."

"FABulous?"

"Yeah he really is!" Sandi managed. For the first time she seemed a little less sure of herself. "Maybe you'd like to see a couple of the cheers we do. That is if you have time. OK?"

"Maybe we will," the interviewer replied. She seemed to look at Sandi with renewed interest. "Why don't you do a couple right now?"

"Really? You really want me to? Right NOW?" Sandi was thrilled! It was happening just the way she had hoped it might. Her picture in a NATIONAL magazine!

"Sure, go ahead. How about over by that backstop?" Miss Crisinski jerked her head toward the two photographers who had accompanied her. They rose and began moving across the gym floor following Sandi. One of them gave the interviewer a wink as he ambled toward the far corner.

"Now maybe we can start again. O.K. Marc?"

"O.K."

The interview and picture session lasted slightly under an hour. Marc was photographed several times, but never in uniform. Sandi leaped and twirled, did splits and everything else she could think of to charm the photographers. Grinning amiably, they fired away, taking shot after shot. She was kept too busy to get back to the interviewer.

Not one picture of the beautiful young cheerleader would ever be seen by anyone.

CHAPTER FIFTEEN

Marc had hardly spoken to his parents all day. He hadn't heard one word the Pastor said in church that morning, and while many congratulated him and wished him well after the service, he had hardly acknowledged them. No one thought it strange, as they assumed he was preoccupied about the all-important contest coming up on Friday.

"Mom!" he yelled from his room, "I need some dark socks."

"Top left drawer, same as always!" she called up the stairs. A minute later she appeared in his doorway. "Are you packing already?" she asked, surprised.

"Have to do SOMETHING," Marc mumbled as he scrabbled around in the bureau.

"Let me get them," Meg sighed, pushing him toward the bed. Marc slumped down by his open suitcase, back bowed and arms hanging beside his knees.

Placing the socks carefully in the half-filled case, she sat down beside him. One hand rested on his shoulder as she looked steadily at her son. "Don't worry so, Marc," she told him, realizing as she did so that there was little she could do or say to help him through these next few days. She knew he had a lot to worry about. His father was much worse, his grades were slipping badly, and he had girlfriend troubles, not to mention the grueling practice schedule and the pressure of playing in Paxton High's first ever state championship.

Forcing a smile she asked, "When does the team bus leave? Wednesday noon did you say?"

Marc did not change his position. "Yeah, Wednesday, There's supposed to be a big pep rally at school in the morning, then leave right after lunch. That way we get three practices in at the Coliseum Wednesday afternoon, Thursday morning, and Thursday afternoon."

"You're going to have THREE PRACTICES before the game Friday night?" Meg was incredulous.

"You know Crites!" Marc replied glumly.

"Well if you have one of your sick spells just tell him you have to miss one of those sessions," Meg told him.

"I never get sick before a game."

Marc's mother looked at him a long moment, worry and concern again causing the lines across her forehead to deepen. Trying once more to cheer him she announced, "Your dad and I have a little surprise planned for you but we can't tell you what it is just yet!"

"Hey Mom, no SURPRISES! OK?"

Meg rubbed Marc's back for a few minutes then rose and left his room.

When he was sure she was downstairs Marc pulled the ragged ARCHAEOLOGY HANDBOOK from under the folded blue jeans in his overnight bag. His hands shook a little as he turned the volume upside down and watched the last white envelope flutter to the floor. He picked it up. Holding it to the light, he studied the unmistakable outline of his last MALO HIERBA leaf resting inside. Suddenly furious, he threw the envelope across the room. One left! Only ONE! Marc held his head and groaned. "What should I do?" he asked himself for the hundredth time. "If I use this one for the semi-finals," he thought, continuing a silent conversation with himself," and we win, I've got none for the championship game. But if I don't use it Friday we might not make it TO the finals." He groaned again, slouched to his feet and retrieved the envelope from under his desk. He shoved it back in the bottom of the suitcase and slammed the lid. "Man it's really great being a sports star!" he sighed.

***

Marcus Cassell was tense. He almost wished the Pacers hadn't earned the bye in the tournament. Waiting out the first round had been harder than playing on that weekend.

The first game of the tournament was exactly twenty minutes away. Still warming up, the Pacers were nervous. Shots were not falling and there had been two embarrassing misses as they muddled through their warm-up circle. The Coliseum at the state capital was huge. All seats had been sold out long before, but the crowd was surprisingly subdued as they watched their teams loosen up. This was for real! No more chances to lose and keep going. Winning tonight would be necessary to advance to the final championship game. The importance of the outcome seemed to lie like a fog over fans and players alike.

Marc shot a glance at the far end of the floor. The competition was awesome. Not only were they tall, they were all husky. "Those guys have spent a lot of time in the weight room," Marc said to Biggy. Both boys held a ball and just watched their opponents for a minute. They looked tough and confident. They were good and they knew it!

Crites walked out on the floor. He stood watching his team for a few minutes then nodded toward the locker room. The team trotted away, leaving Crites and Jamison to follow down the carpeted hallway to their dressing room.

Crites stood by the door. He seemed to be examining the lush facilities. It was the first time he had brought a team far enough to play at state. No one spoke. They sat watching their coaches, waiting.

"Nelson, what do you have to say?" Crites asked quietly, taking the big man completely by surprise.

"We've got to win it," the center answered, rising to the occasion.

"Cassell?"

Marc gulped. He knew this was no time for a joke, but one half of his last MALO HIERBA was rolling through his system and he wanted badly to laugh. "The films showed us what we're up against," he said. He couldn't help grinning a little, "but we can take them. We've got to!"

"How's your dad doing?" ? Crites asked conversationally.

Marc leaned forward, his hands clasped together below his knees. "O.K. I guess," he replied. He wondered what Crites was up to. Also he didn't want to think about his father right now. The grin that had been lurking along the side of his mouth had disappeared.

Crites made the rounds, asking seemingly strange questions of each player. They answered in a word or two, glancing uneasily at each other. Finally he finished. There was hardly anytime left and the boys were getting anxious to get on with it.

"You are the finest team I have ever coached. You can win this game and you WILL win it. I KNOW it! And you also know that I have never EVER predicted a win before a game. This time I am because I am that sure." He held the door open. "Go on out there," he said, not even raising his voice, "and get us past this one and into the finals."

Marc was smiling openly now. Crites was not a well-liked coach but he knew how to motivate kids! He had effectively cut through the nervous jitters created by a huge playing arena, fancy dressing rooms, and thousands of fans. It was, he had shown them, just another game not unlike any of the others they had already played.

***

It was a toss-up between Nelson and Cassell. No one could name the better player in the semi-finals. Marc and Biggy accounted for 66 of their team's final ninety-one points. The Pacers amazed everyone by clubbing their excellent opponent by twenty points.

Next stop, the State Championship!

***

Once again Marc found himself in his *thinking* position. Head lolling at the foot of his bed, his long, skinny legs angled upward until both heels rested on the headboard.

For once he felt pretty good for a Monday. The nausea had been bad Saturday morning however. The long bus ride from the capital back to Paxton had been a night-mare! The team and cheerleaders had screamed and cheered nearly all the way. Because of their impressive win, Crites had allowed the cheerleaders to ride home in the team bus. At every small town the bus windows had been thrown open in spite of the blowing snow. Players had yelled themselves hoarse at the few grinning passers-by still up at this hour. Marc had huddled under his varsity jacket, sick and miserable. Twice Sandi had tried to get him to join the fun, but being unsuccessful, had cheered her way to the front of the bus and plopped down on Mickey Beeler's lap. She had not spoken to Marc since then.

***

The house was quiet, but outside the wind moaned as it rounded the corner of his room on the second floor. School was closed due to the storm which had come roaring in from the southwest on Sunday. It had brought heavy drifting snow which soon had the country roads impassible.

Marc's bedside clock read slightly after ten before the wind appeared to be slackening.

"Too bad Crites!" Marc yelled aloud. "No school – no practice! That's school policy!"

It was nice to be alone in his room on a no-school Monday. He was thankful that his mother, having heard the weather predictions, had decided to go to the hospital and stay overnight with Paul. She would probably not try to get home for at least another day to allow time for the roads to be cleared.

The phone rang twice before Marc wakened. He hadn't realized he was asleep again.

"Hi Marc. How you doing?" It was Susan. Her voice sounded polite but that was all.

"Hey Susan. I'm great. No school, no practice, no PROBLEM! What's happening with you?"

There was long pause, then politely again, "How is your dad doing?"

"He's still in the hospital. Mom doesn't say much, but when I go to see him he really looks beat. I guess he's in the best place for him right now though. Mom stayed over at the hospital last night. I'm all alone here and I'm scared the BOOGEY MAN will get me!"

Susan ignored his lame attempt at humor and there was another long pause. "I suppose you saw a lot of our head cheerleader after the game Friday night." Susan's voice had taken on a hard note. "How was the bus ride home on Saturday?" she continued. "I'll bet you two had a great time together THEN!"

"I was so sick I hardly knew what was going on!" Marc growled into the phone. "Is this why you called? You wanted to give me a hard time?"

"O. K. Marc," Susan began, "I just need to know where we stand. Are you and I through or what?"

Marc was angry. "Are you giving me an ultimatum here? It has to yes or no right NOW? As far as I'm concerned nothing has changed at all. You know Sandi. She flirts with everybody. Mickey told me she sat on his lap all the way home Saturday."

"All right then," Susan replied. Marc could tell she was crying again. "I just need ed to know that's all. Can you come over after while? Mom couldn't go to work today but Dad left early so I guess he got there O.K."

Marc glanced out the kitchen window. "No way Sus," he answered, "my car could never make it. Maybe I could come over after practice tomorrow. That is if we have school." *Marc was extremely grateful that his parents had finally agreed that he was no longer to be grounded.*

"That would be nice Marc. Please come!" She was almost sobbing by this time. "Bye."

Marc stood at the kitchen window and watched a snowdrift building around the empty dog house in the back yard. Why do things always have to get so complicated, he wondered. With a tired sigh he opened the refrigerator and began pulling out a few items for his lunch. As soon as the wind stopped completely he would have to clear the drive. He looked forward to the physical activity. When shoveling snow you could tell if you were making progress. With girls ... well you just never knew.

***

Assistant coach Jamison finally thrust both hands high above his head, but the screaming and stomping hardly diminished. The gym was packed, not only with the entire high school student body, but it seemed nearly half the adult population of the village of Paxton had crowded in. The pep rally the week before had been memorable, but this was fantastic!

The cheerleaders, ably led by captain Sandi Myles, ignored Jamison's pleas for quiet and kept the cheering block in a constant uproar. The assistant coach shrugged his shoulders, sort of gave up, and just stood by the microphone grinning. Surprisingly, seeing this, the crowd began to settle down a little.

When it was finally reasonably quiet, Jamison still did not speak. Turning slightly he let his gaze rest briefly on every Paxton varsity player. Wearing matching blazers, dark blue trousers, and blue and white striped ties, the team sat on a single row of chairs behind the podium. Facing their adoring fans, most of them managed to look humble, but confident.

"Ladies and gentlemen," Jamison said, turning into the microphone, "may I present to you our team members. The next state champions!" As one person the fans surged to their feet screaming and clapping. There was pandemonium again. First it was just noise, but with the cheerleaders' help the crowd gradually fell into a unison chant; PACERS. PACERS. PACERS!

Jamison turned to those behind him and shook his head. There was nothing to do but wait. The cheering and chanting continued for a full three minutes before gradually dying down.

When it was finally quiet again the Mayor of Paxton was introduced. Wisely, he kept his remarks brief and positive. Biggy's father, representing the booster club, was next. He was greeted with thunderous applause which threatened to halt the proceedings again. One huge raised palm brought the crowd under control quickly. He praised the school, the fans, and the players, but used most of his time to compliment the coaches. He reminded all present that good coaching was what it took to weld a bunch of boys into a winning team.

Superintendent Flores spoke briefly, exhorting the team members and fans to be good representatives of their fine school and community. He urged them to conduct themselves honorably at the state capital, since their actions would be observed by large numbers of people. He sat down, slightly surprised at the applause which followed his remarks.

Mr. Seeks, high school principal, looked pointedly at his watch, then pretending to glare into the crowd, remarked, "We should get back to class SOON!" Boos and cat-calls shouted him down at once. "Kidding! Just KIDDING," he laughed into the microphone as the boos turned into cheers and whistles.

When Seeks finished he asked both coaches to come forward. The cheering erupted again and continued for more than a minute. Jamison spoke first.

"This is my tenth year at Paxton," he began, "and it's been the best ten years of my life (cheering again)! For the past eight of those years I've been privileged to work with some fine young men and women (More cheers). But beyond that I count myself lucky to have the honor of assisting one of the finest coaches in our state! I give you Coach Weldon Crites, maker of CHAMPIONS!"

The standing ovation affected Crites in a way that surprised even him. Appalled, he felt tears filling his eyes. He knew beyond a doubt that he was not well liked by Paxton students. He was also painfully aware that his health and physical education classes were dreaded by many of them. Yet here they were showing him honor which he knew he did not deserve at all. He felt a tear slide down his cheek.

"Thank you," he managed. He touched his cheek with a curled forefinger. He had trouble continuing. Clearing his throat noisily into the microphone he made a sweeping gesture at the line of well scrubbed, blue-coated Pacers behind him. "They made it happen (pandemonium)!"

When the fans finally began taking their seats again Crites surprised everyone there by his next actions. Leaving the microphone behind he walked slowly toward the community members packed along all of the sidelines in the hot and overcrowded gym.

Extending his hand he half pulled a pretty, young looking lady out onto the floor. In the quiet that followed him he did not need the sound system.

"Like Coach Jamison said I owe a lot of people. But I want you to meet the person who means the most to me. My wife, Julie."

The applause was adequate but subdued. Coach Crites always kept everyone guessing. It was one of the secrets of his success. Students sitting through his admittedly boring classes or watching his antics with the ball club had hardly considered that he was also a married man who had a life apart from school and sports. They looked at them both with new respect.

Half pulling his embarrassed wife with him, Crites returned to the podium. Still holding her by the hand he leaned close to the microphone, pointed left, and shouted, "There's your TEAM!"

The boys stood up, proud and tall in the matching blazers recently supplied by the Paxton Merchants' Association. The pep band ripped into a frenzied rendition of the Pacer Fight Song as two thousand pairs of lungs added to the acclaim. The noise was deafening. The fans were LOVING it!

It's hard to say how long this would have continued had not Jamison jerked a thumb toward Punchy Markles. He limped forward and raised both hands for attention. Although out of action, he was still team captain and a very popular student.

Lifting the microphone from its standard he gazed solemnly into the sea of expectant faces before him. "I can't understand how they got this far without ME!" The gym exploded in laughter. What a character he was! He replaced the mic, limped back to his seat, made a sweeping bow to his teammates and sat down. Applause and laughter continued.

Biggy's blazer was too small. This made him appear even larger than he was. When he got the nod from Jamison he removed the jacket and draped it carefully over the back of his chair. The sleeves touched the floor.

The fans laughed as the big center raised the microphone as high as it would go, then hunched down to get his mouth close enough. His shaved head gleamed with sweat. He was more nervous now than he had been in the semi-finals last week!

"We got a real TEAM here," he began. "Coach and us, we work together. Sometimes we get mad, but when we do we just take it out on the OTHER TEAMS!" Cheers and clapping interrupted him. "We're proud to be Pacers!"

As Biggy ambled toward his seat Coach Jamison was surprised to see Mr. Nelson, Biggy's father, striding up to the microphone. His second appearance was not in the schedule that had been planned for this final pep session.

Almost as tall as his son, Mr. Nelson leaned over the podium. "Excuse me for interrupting these fine proceedings," he said, "but I think you would want to know what my son Benjamin didn't tell you. Last night about ten o'clock he signed a letter of intent to play basketball at State next year (another standing ovation)!

Clapping along with the crowd, Jamison re-claimed command. "We've got one more person to hear from, then we've got to get these boys and girls into the buses and on their way! This guy keeps us all guessing. He's had his ups and downs this season, but there's no doubt in my mind that without him we wouldn't be playing in the state coliseum on Friday! Ladies and gentlemen I give you Paxton's claim-to-fame, the Never-Miss-Kid (stomping, whistles, and cheers)!

Marc's mind was in a whirl. They were all expecting another twenty or thirty point game from him in the finals. His picture was plastered all over the papers. TV reporters, some even from neighboring states, were asking for interviews (Crites had of course for-bidden any of these until after the championship game). As he slowly ambled toward the speaker's stand all these thoughts were flashing through his brain. But the one which had plagued him right up until this moment was that there were no MALO HIERBA leaves left. None! They were all counting on him and he was going to blow it. As he took his place to speak he had never, ever felt more miserable.

"I want to thank a lot of people. Our coaches, the team, the business men downtown who got us these outfits, our parents who put up with us (laughter) our teachers (groans) and we don't want to forget our CHEERLEADERS (wolf whistles and applause) and most of all, I thank God for HIS help in getting us this far."

Marc had known he would be asked to speak, so he'd thought a lot about what he should say. But all at once now he couldn't remember what he had planned to do next. "I, uh ..." Suddenly Marc noticed that many of the fans were no longer looking at him. Twisting in their seats they were staring off toward the lobby. Tears sprang into his eyes as once more the crowd came quietly to their feet as Meg Cassell pushed Paul's wheelchair into the gym. Marc's speech was over and so was the pep session.

Forty minutes later the buses ground their way out of the school parking lot as fans lined the alleys and cheered them on.

It had been a morning none of them would ever forget!

CHAPTER SIXTEEN

It was a very quiet trip to the capital. Crites had not actually forbidden the usual horseplay, but the few times it had started he had slowly turned from the front seat and given one of his famous *looks*! It was clear he expected them to keep their minds on the championship game which was only two days away.

Marc stared out of the window, watching the snow-covered countryside slide by. Beeler sprawled beside him, apparently sound asleep. Marcus was angry at almost everyone, but mostly at himself. *"Why did I use that leaf in the semi-finals?"* he asked himself for the hundredth time. There was no answer. The last MALO HIERBA had done its work and there were no more.

Marc knew he had to make a decision and the sooner he made it the better it would be for the team. As it stood now he would certainly be the starting point guard. But without the boost from his magical leaves he felt certain he would hardly be able to do the job they had learned to expect from him. On the other hand the team's major offensive strategy was built around Biggy and him. If Crites had to change things around now it could throw everything into a dangerous state of confusion.

Eyes closed, Marc bumped his head softly against the cold bus window. Here he was, living the sort of adventure that was every prep school basketball player's dream and he was miserable! Finally he decided to talk with Coach Jamison. But then he realized that the assistant coach was on the other bus! He just couldn't bring himself to confide in Coach Crites. Not TODAY anyway!

Typically for a seventeen-year-old, Marc did nothing but continue to worry.

THE KID WHO COULDN'T MISS

***

"MOVE Cassell!" Crites roared, slapping his clipboard against his thigh. Eyes narrowed, he watched as his Never-Miss-Kid was late on still another pass and screen play. Shaking his head angrily the coach forced himself to swallow the tirade he would normally have laid on Marcus Cassell.

"That KID," he growled to Jamison, shaking his head. "He's dead on his feet out there. It's throwing everyone's timing off. How can a guy look so bad in practice then when he gets in a game. well you know."

"He's got problems coach," Jamison said softly.

"Yeah his dad's critical again now they say. It took guts for Paul Cassell to come to that pep session, but it was probably a mistake."

"Well," Jamison replied, "that's ONE of his problems but I don't think it's the biggest one he's got right now."

Crites blew a sharp blast on his whistle. "Five minutes!" he bellowed. "Go easy on the water!" As the team trotted toward the recessed fountains at each end of the huge facility he turned to Jamison.

"You don't mean Cassell has girl problems?" he snorted. Disgust drew his mouth into a scowl.

"I wish it was that simple. Coach, I'm almost sure the kid is taking something that peps him up right before a game."

"Do you think I'm BLIND?" Crites asked incredulously. "I've suspected that for half the season at least. And I'll bet at least some of the fans do too. But back in November I did a little detective work. Not one of the blood tests Doc Shelton or their family doctor, Bennett, did showed a single thing. If he's into something it's one nobody knows about! The police pathology lab people couldn't understand it either. After that accident they said he showed all the signs, but nothing showed up in any of their tests."

"Do you plan to keep on letting him do this stuff?"

Crites threw his towel on the floor angrily. "What do you expect me to DO? Accuse the kid right out? His old man's dying, his grades are so low he's just barely eligible, and he's so banged up physically the trainer has to practically tape him together so he can play! Jamison nodded, staring up into the ranks of empty seats.

"But Coach." Jamison began.

"Look," Crites interrupted, "let's not forget what's going to happen tomorrow night. It's the championship right? Whatever Cassell is doing he's been at it all season. I've tried to find out what it is, but so far I haven't been able to. So now I'm saying we let it ride until it's over here in the coliseum."

"O.K. I'm with you coach."

"One more thing." Crites lowered his voice. The team was forming up, ready to go again. "Why do think the kid didn't get that scholarship to State? Biggy got one, which was no surprise to anybody, but not Cassell. They're afraid of him that's why. But you can bet your last dollar they wouldn't say anything about WHY!"

One short blast of his whistle brought the stragglers hurrying back on the floor. Crites made two substitutions from his second string in order to keep all twelve players loose. He also wanted each and every one, even those who had hardly been in a game all season, to believe they were important and that they had a real chance of seeing action in the championship game.

The Pacers had never looked so sharp. Every uniform was cleaned and pressed. Their satin warm-up jackets and pants were navy blue with white piping. There were no beards and no hair long enough to distract a player's concentration. Crites had had his battles over these rules, but he had held the line. There had been few complaints during the last two seasons.

The Paxton team had soon become used to the plush facilities provided for teams in the state finals. Individual shower stalls, deep carpet in the conference room, recessed lighting, none of it impressed them anymore. Six practice sessions and two games and they felt themselves deserving of such luxury!

"Would all the seniors please stand?" Crites asked quietly. His tie, though it clashed with his jacket, was neatly tied for once. He had new shoes. The eight seniors came to their feet slowly, glancing uneasily at each other while avoiding eye contact with their coach.

"Boys, this will be the last time you'll have to listen to old Crites chew your tails (they grinned)! "That is unless I EVER hear of any of you messing up anytime, anywhere during the next forty years (laughter)!"

"You juniors don't know what you're in for!" Biggy said, rolling his eyes. Jamison was cracking up and even Crites laughed a little.

"You've made me proud of you. I know I've been hard on you. Real hard. I did what I thought I had to do to get OUT of you what's inside. You're going to have to deal with tough guys and tough situations from now on. Trials and problems don't stop when the season ends. They don't stop when you graduate either. If you've learned anything of value playing for me these past four years I hope it's this; when it's tough you get tougher, when you get knocked down, get up again. And most of all I hope you've learned that you have WORTH. You're YOU. There's no one else. You're WINNERS (they cheered)!"

Crites slowly lowered himself onto the high stool before the chalkboard.

The seniors, not sure what was expected, continued to stand. Crites got up then. He hitched up his belt and moved over to Mickey Beeler. Opening his arms he drew the skinny black forward into a bear hug. Tears streaming unheeded down his cheeks, he made the rounds. Most of the players were choked up too. How could they have hated this man? What could they do for him that would be enough to show their gratitude and love?

Crites did not neglect the juniors either. Each one got a hug.

Jamison followed their head coach, grabbing arms and slapping backs but there was no way he could move these young men the way the head coach had done.

"Sit down. Sit down." Crites blew his nose noisily and dabbed at his eyes. He sniffed mightily. "Now Jamison and I have a little surprise for you guys." He jerked his head toward the elaborate office complex that was his to use during the championship game. Jamison opened the door with a flourish.

"Let's hear it for ME!" It was Punchy Markles! He was in uniform and was walking without crutches. Heavy tape showed well above his left sock.

His astonished teammates howled in delight.

"You gonna PLAY, man?" Biggy's eyes were nearly popping from his head. "Sure I'm playing. Right Coach?"

Crites nodded. "He's been working out on the sly for almost a month now and we think he's READY. I didn't want anybody to know he was going back on the starting five tonight. He's our secret weapon! This should really mess up Central Valley's defense. Markles ain't in one of the game films Central's been studying all week!" Crites slapped his thigh with the ever present clipboard and laughed aloud as the team whistled and crowded around the strutting senior in surprise. Crites had done it again!

***

Marcus Cassell was feeling a little better now. With Punchy back in the line-up he would not be expected to carry so much of the offensive load.

There was a greater reason for his lightened mood however. For the first time during the entire season he felt like HIMSELF! He could remember every word of Crites' pre-game pep talk. He did not have to fight the need to laugh at everything, funny or not. But most of all he knew that whatever happened in this game, or for the rest of his life, it would be what he could do himself. It would not be happening because of some crazy weed from Central America which made you into something you were never intended to be! He was genuinely glad all the MALO HIERBA leaves were gone.

Their warm-up drill brought the Pacer fans to their feet clapping and stamping their feet in unison. The ball zipped around the circle like a meteor as twelve blue clad Pacers spiraled ever closer and closer to the basket. When they were shoulder to shoulder the ball was lobbed high and Biggy erupted for his trade mark two-handed slam. The voices of nearly ten thousand Paxton fans roared in delight.

Crites motioned and the team slipped out of their warm-up suits. They closed around him, eager faces attuned, ready for his last minute instructions.

"Well men this is what we came for It's now or never, there's no more chances after tonight." His voice was surprisingly calm. He was still wearing his jacket, and hadn't even loosened his tie. "Play your own game, don't let them make you play theirs!"

"Hey guys," Punchy said, his face deadly serious, "remember; don't shoot until you have the ball!" Everyone, even Crites lost it. Fans near enough stared incredulously at twelve kids and two adults LAUGHING just moments before the boys' state championship finals! Crites and Jamison shoved their arms into the center of the circle. The players' hands, black and white alike, piled on top.

"Do it!" Crites whispered. The starting five broke away to join Central Valley East already in position.

The referee lofted the ball and the game was under way.

The gold-suited Central players were cautious but confident. They scored on a carefully executed screen play, then electrified their fans by nearly stealing the ball on Paxton's in-bounds pass. They worked the ball expertly and in less than one minute had scored again.

Punchy Markles, always the strutting, self-confident player, was obviously nervous. He had been getting his ankle in shape but had not practiced with the team in a long while. Finding his usual unconscious timing slightly off, he felt rattled and unsure. Marc could see it would be up to him to take charge, at least until Punchy had time to settle into the game. Faking his defender neatly he took the pass from Beeler and dribbled down the sideline toward the Paxton basket. Whipping the ball to Punchy he cut across the center to take the return pass. Faking a shot he fired the ball deep into the corner, Beeler whipped it behind his back to Biggy who had position on his defender. Biggy dropped it in and Paxton was on the scoreboard.

Central held the ball as long as possible, attempting to slow the game down. Their coach was well aware of the scoring punch provided by the huge Paxton center, but he was more concerned with the guard everyone was now talking about. The Never-Miss-Kid had astonished him as he and his team watched the films of the Pacers' last few games. His scouting reports had also warned of the potentially devastating effect of this kid's ability to hit from anywhere on the floor.

"Slow the game down!" the Central coach had hammered into them all week. "They can't score while WE'VE got the ball!" Well disciplined, his team was following his game plan to the letter. By taking only the best shots and keeping the ball moving fast around the perimeter they were definitely in charge. Four minutes into the game they were ahead 14-9.

Crites signaled for a time out.

"How's the ankle?" he asked Punchy.

"It's O.K. coach. Doesn't even hurt."

"Good! O.K. You and Cassell trade places then. I want Marc on point. You drop back more. Help out underneath. Both of you guys use the trap on their number thirty-two. Tie him up if you can.

"Cassell," he snapped, take some shots from outside. We've got to pull them out on you to loosen their defense. They've got Nelson bottled up under there. We need to score too. And Marc .... no CRAZY stuff, OK?"

"Sure Coach!" Marc yelled as the huddle broke.

"Don't worry Crites," Marc thought, "believe me I'm not feeling one bit crazy tonight!"

Crites's plan made sense. With Cassell handling the ball out front Markles was free to cut and run. It worked well for several minutes' playing time. Marc had been left wide open several times for the long one-handers that he especially liked. He had scored once but missed twice. His passing got the ball in to Biggy regularly but the big center was still having to fight to get his shots away. Central had two men nearly as tall as he and one a good two inches taller. Still he bulled his way to the basket and made three shots close in.

Central continued their conservative play. Their intimidating size allowed them almost complete control of the boards. When they did miss one of their shots their re-bounders usually managed to tap it in.

Punchy was hurting. Marc knew all the signs. Markles was not getting back nearly fast enough on defense. He had only scored twice, both of these from long range. The injured ankle was slowing him down more with each minute of play. Defensively he began to lose his opponent more and more often. Picking up on this immediately, Central began running plays through his area regularly.

The quarter ended with Central fans on their feet cheering. With twenty-nine points on the scoreboard they led the Pacers by ten.

Crites had his jacket off now! His tie hung loose and his face was rapidly becoming the blotchy red that players and fans knew so well.

"J.J. go in for Markles," he yelled. Grabbing Marc by the arm he glared at him, their faces only inches apart. "You have to shoot more. When you're open, put it UP man! If biggy ain't open look to the sides. Beeler is getting free in the corner quite a bit. Drive in there, pull them out on you! Got that?"

"O.K. Coach. Want me to take the point again?"

"Yeah. And for once in your life do what I tell you!" Crites talked desperately, trying to set a program that would halt the strangle hold that Central maintained under the basket.

Play resumed.

Coach Jamison tore his eyes away from the game long enough to take a good look at Punchy. The boy was breathing hard. Two pale spots showed high on his cheekbones. He sat straight up, his left leg extended before him. Jamison was shocked as for the first time he noticed the ugly bulge pushing out all around the top of the heavy tape.

Jamison jerked his head toward the trainer and pointed at Punchy's leg. The assistant coach had a good idea of what the trainer's recommendation would be. Of course it was still up to the head coach to decide if Markles could get back in the game.

The Pacers looked bad. Punchy's replacement was so nervous he got rid of the ball as if it were red hot. Cassell, the "Never-Miss-Kid," might as well have been called the "Never-HIT-Kid." Fans from either side of the field house could not believe it.

Following his coach's orders, Marc fired the ball up whenever he was open. He made one shot while missing four times. Fortunately,

Central was still worried about his scoring potential. Pulling their defense well out to cover him had the effect Crites wanted. Marc's passing was still adequate. Biggy and Beeler were starting to score underneath.

The half ended with Central still on top. Paxton had given it all they had but still trailed by nine.

Loyal Paxton fans gave the Pacers a standing ovation as they trooped toward their dressing rooms. While not playing well it was obvious to everyone in the coliseum that they had not given up. Half the game was still to come!

Marc, on his way to the dressing room, was suddenly startled as a slight figure squeezed through the angled railing beside the ramp.

"Marc!"

It was Susan.

"Here," she whispered urgently, jamming a tightly folded square of paper into his sweaty palm.

Before he could speak she had dashed up the ramp and vanished into the milling crowd.

Crites' anger was apparent to all. They sensed however that he was not faulting the team. Rather the rage he felt was against circumstances. *Why did Punchy have to get a serious injury early in the season? Why tonight of ALL nights, did the famous "Never-Miss-Kid have to be shooting a terrible twenty-five percent?*

Fighting his surging emotions Coach Crites turned to the chalkboard and quickly sketched a new plan for the second half. It was a desperate attempt, but to continue as they were meant a certain loss.

'MARKLES," he barked, slashing a circle well down in the corner of the court diagram, "I'm putting you in at forward. Hang back in the corners and take your shots every time you're open! Beeler, try to cover for him getting back on defense since he's slowed down with that leg."

"Cassell, you've got to get more passes in to Nelson. And Biggy, go to your left more so you can see when Marc's sending one in."

Crites went on, desperately dealing with his plans for the remainder of the game. Coach Jamison, standing slightly behind

Biggy and Markles, could hardly take his eyes off Punchy's leg. The swelling had no place to go except above the tape circling halfway up his calf It had become noticeably worse during the second quarter and now extended all the way to his knee. Jamison made his decision.

"Coach," he interrupted quietly, "you better have the trainer take a good look at his leg." He nodded toward Punchy who was giving him an angry look. "There's no way he's going to be able to run the length of the floor every time the ball changes hands. Maybe out front he could handle it but."

Crites' face was turning crimson. He choked back a furious reply. "What about it Markles? Can you do it or not?"

"I think so Coach. but I'm slow and..." This was not the cocky ball player they all knew. Crites could tell as well as anyone that the kid was willing but unable.

"O.K., O.K. then," Crites' shoulders slumped. He chewed viciously at his lower lip, then whirled to the chalkboard once more. "Markles, you sit out the third quarter at least. Ice your ankle down and re-tape it good. If your leg feels good enough and we need you we'll go with this plan starting fourth quarter. OK?"

Suddenly Marc rose to his feet and started sidling toward the restroom. "Sorry Coach!" he murmured as he hurried away.

As Crites rapidly gave more instructions, Coach Jamison eased away toward the half open door where Marcus Cassell had disappeared. He stopped just short of the opening and watched.

Marc slipped the little packet out of its hiding place and stared at it. Wrapped in notebook paper and sealed with a single piece of tape, it looked innocent enough. Nothing was written on it. Marc knew that whatever he did in the next moment would affect not only his life but the lives of his teammates, coaches, and many others. Perhaps with the help of this last MALO HIERBA leaf he could stave off the disaster that this game could become. On the other hand the weed was no good. It had messed him up in so many ways. Would he want other athletes to find out about it? They would be certain to use it regardless of the harm it would do.

Marc watched as his fingers, seemingly working without his direction, popped the tape and unfolded the paper surrounding the little pile of dry brown leaf. He smiled as he noticed a few pieces of lint and pink fuzz mixed in with the leaf fragments. *"Susan's jacket pocket,"* he thought.

Heaving a great sigh, he watched as his hand turned over and the brown bits fluttered gently down and spread across the surface of the water. He touched the lever and watched as a very large part of his young life swirled away forever.

Stepping out the door he was surprised to see a grinning Coach Jamison blocking his path. The assistant grabbed him by both arms and whispered, "That's the best decision you'll ever make!" Marc wasn't so sure. He hurried back to the team. There was still half a game to play and the outcome would depend largely on him.

"Well," Marc told himself as they mounted the stairs, "Whatever I do it will be ME, not some drug!"

***

Just before he was ready to send the team back to the court, Crites decided to revise his game plan again! The changes were important, but as a result of the lost time the team was late getting back to the game and a technical foul was called. Paxton went down another point!

Marc was feeling good. His aching joints had eased some during the halftime break. His mind was clear. He remembered every word his coach had said. But most of all he felt more and more as if he had done the right thing. Coach Jamison's whispered compliment seemed to repeat itself in his mind as he took position for the tip-off.

Punchy was needed. It soon became apparent that with the little general on the bench Central had adjusted their defense to close in even harder on the big men underneath. Marc knew what this meant. Crites would be begging for some of those spectacular, long range one-handers which had brought the crowd to its feet so many times during the season. The lanky guard set himself, but faked the shot and rammed a slider in to Beeler. The shot was a *groane*r which rolled nearly all the way around the rim. Biggy went up with the taller

Central center, but was unable to tap it in. Central took the re-bound, lost it, gained it back in a scramble, then finally managed to get it down court. Marc shadowed his man, keeping one hand in his face and the other deceptively low. At the moment his opponent attempted to pass it off, Marc's left hand flew up and slapped the ball away. He scooped it up and dribbled the length of the court. Defenders were all over him but he managed to lay it up and in. He drew a foul in the process and sank it too.

The two teams were not evenly matched. Paxton, even though noted for its bench strength back in the Tri-lakes league, was up against real depth on this final game of the season. No one could have played harder than the Pacers. Crites used up all his time outs.

Late in the fourth quarter the coach ran Punchy Markles back into the game. Within two minutes it was obvious that the tough little guard could not hold up. Crites yanked him out again as his blue-clad teammates continued to fall behind.

Marcus Cassell, without the aid of his secret drug, scored twenty-three points. He improved considerably in the second half, shooting a very respectable forty-two percent from the field. Biggy Nelson, the individual scoring champion of his home region, added another thirty-one to his total for the year, and was named *most valuable player* in the game.

Paxton lost eighty-seven to seventy-five.

Marcus Cassell, the Never-Miss-Kid while playing on the losing team, was a winner in the truest sense of the word. He had won the hardest battle of all; he had won the victory over SELF!

***

The bus hummed its way down the interstate. They were going home. The light snow which was falling seemed to fit their mood. The team members talked quietly or slept. The runner-up trophy rested between the coaches on the front seat. It was after one o'clock a.m.

Marc turned to Punchy. "How's the leg?"

"Hurts!" Markles replied.

Marcus leaned back against the head rest. "Know what I'm going to do tomorrow?"

"Sleep?" Punchy answered.

"Nope," Marc continued.

"Call Susan and play kissy-kissy over the phone?"

"Nope."

"O.K. I get it NOW. You're gonna go see Miss Sandi Myles, right?"

"Not that either."

"Well," Punchy growled, "what then?"

"Tomorrow," Cassell said, "first I'm going to sit down and talk to my dad for at least an HOUR. And then I'm actually going to change the oil in Mom's car!"

THE END

Printed in the United States
63298LVS00002B/133-156